SNOWFLAKES OVER THE SECOND CHANCES SWEET SHOP

HANNAH LYNN

Boldwood

First published in Great Britain in 2024 by Boldwood Books Ltd.

Cover Design by Alexandra Allden

Cover Photography: Shutterstock

A CIP catalogue record for this book is available from the British Library.

Paperback ISBN 978-1-83603-771-2

Large Print ISBN 978-1-83603-772-9

Harback ISBN 978-1-83603-770-5

Ebook ISBN 978-1-83603-773-6

Kindle ISBN 978-1-83603-774-3

Audio CD ISBN 978-1-83603-765-1

MP3 CD ISBN 978-1-83603-766-8

Digital audio download ISBN 978-1-83603-769-9

Boldwood Books Ltd
23 Bowerdean Street
London SW6 3TN
www.boldwoodbooks.com

To Kim Barlow and Wendy Neels, who have been with Holly since the beginning.
Thank you for all your support.

1

Jamie picked a bar of coconut ice off the shelf and promptly unwrapped it.

'You know, I'm sure it's going to be this Christmas,' she said, before taking her first sugary mouthful of the sweet. 'I can feel it. Evan is going to propose to you this Christmas.'

Rather than responding straight away, Holly focused on weighing up a large bag of aniseed balls that Jamie had requested. Since falling pregnant, Jamie's sweet tooth had increased no end, and some days, Holly was sure her friend spent more time in the sweet shop than she did.

'Evan and I are fine as we are,' Holly said. She scooped out another handful of the shiny red balls. In Holly's opinion, a life-time supply of sweets seemed more than fair, given everything Jamie had done for her since she moved back to Bourton. It wasn't just that she was Holly's best friend, had offered her a place to live, and been happy for her to stay, even with a new-born baby. Without Jamie and Fin, Holly never would have met Evan, and now here they were, a year and a half later, going stronger than ever.

A lot of things had happened since Holly met Evan at his villa in France, the biggest of which being the pair had bought a house together in the small village of Clapton-on-the-Hill, just outside Bourton. It had been a fixer-upper. And that was putting it nicely. The entire place had needed gutting, with new flooring, bathroom, kitchen, and practically every other feature in the place, too. In fact, the only things that were the same as when they'd looked around were the fireplaces. It had been a slog, particularly with Hope getting into everything, walking, talking, and generally wanting as much attention as possible, and Evan still having to fly off around the world to keep his business running.

But they had got there, and moved in together only three weeks ago, giving them plenty of time to get settled in before Christmas, when, for the first time ever, Holly was going to host. With Jamie pregnant, numerous children in attendance and Caroline's eldest daughter at the age where she loved nothing more than looking after Hope, it was bound to be a special day. Ben and Georgia were also coming, as was Giles. Along with Holly's parents.

But there was one set of guests that Holly was even more excited (although possibly a little nervous) to meet, and that was Evan's parents, who were flying in from Seattle. It was going to be a full house, and Holly didn't need a proposal to make her life with Evan perfect. It already was.

'You know we're happy as we are,' she said, reinforcing her point to Jamie. 'I don't need a ring. Besides, I don't know why you're saying all this stuff, anyway. If Evan was going to propose, he would've already told Fin, and Fin would've told you.'

She screwed the lid on the jar containing the aniseed balls and placed them back on the shelf.

Jamie pressed her lips tightly together. 'I know, I thought that too. I don't get it. I think maybe Fin is just not telling me things because he's worried if I get too excited, it'll send me into early labour.'

'Or maybe he's just not telling you things because there's nothing to tell,' Holly responded. 'Now, is there anything else you want, or have you just come in to distract me all day?'

'Mainly to distract you. I'm not so good at this maternity leave thing. I thought I'd quite like it. You know, plenty of time to relax and chill and do my own thing. But it's really difficult. I'm used to being so active. You should've seen Fin's face when I said I wanted to go for a bike ride. I swear if he could, he'd have me sitting in front of the television with my feet up and blankets over me until this baby is born.'

Holly had to chuckle. Jamie was right. Considering his outgoing lifestyle, and the way both he and Jamie approached all adventures in life, Fin had become incredibly cautious the moment they found out about the pregnancy. So much so that he'd insisted Jamie cut back on work. Or at least tasks that involved her climbing up and down ladders and fixing people's roofs. Jamie had protested for quite a while, on the account that she'd never had an accident before, and saw no reason for it to change just because she was pregnant, but when the bump started growing, shifting her centre of balance, and she found it harder to fit her tool belt around her waist, she finally conceded, much to Fin's relief. It was sweet, though, how excited he was. And soon Jamie would have a baby, and Holly wouldn't put it past Ben and Georgia to start trying soon too. Holly and her friends were all in this incredible place of life at the same time.

'You know, Evan doesn't have to propose for you to start thinking about having children together,' Jamie said, breaking Holly's stream of thoughts. 'You already know from Hope what an amazing dad he'd be.'

Holly didn't respond, but only because Jamie had vocalised

the very thought that had just entered her head. She and Evan had talked about having more children together, but they'd wanted to wait until the house was sorted. Now that was done, there was nothing stopping them. Unless, of course, it had just been a delay tactic by Evan, and he wasn't quite as keen as he first appeared. If that was the case, Holly couldn't blame him; after all, the start of their relationship had been intense enough as it was. Wanting a little downtime was probably natural.

Although Jamie was right about one thing: Evan was incredible with Hope. The pair adored each other, and anyone who saw them together would assume he was her biological father. Hope even called his parents Granny and Grandad whenever they called on the phone – though Evan had asked Holly's permission first, and she'd agreed with barely a second thought. She and Evan were in this forever and when they did have children together, the last thing she wanted was for Hope to feel separate from the rest of his family. So referring to Evan's parents as an extra set of grandparents made sense. Especially as they were so keen.

It was only when Jamie cleared her throat that Holly realised she'd been standing there for quite some time without responding.

'We'll see,' she said, which provoked a suitable smirk from Jamie.

'Right, I guess I should be off,' Jamie said, swinging her bag over her shoulder. 'I'm going to one of those antenatal yoga classes they've got going at the gym. You know, the type where you sit on the balls and have to breathe in and out ridiculously slowly?'

Holly knew the classes very well. She remembered them clearly from her days with Hope, though she couldn't see herself doing them again – if she and Evan were to get pregnant.

'Well, have fun. I'll see you later?' Holly asked. There was barely an evening that went by when they didn't see one another.

'Of course.'

'Love you.'

'Love you too. And remember, I need to be the first person you call when Evan proposes.'

Holly shook her head and let out a groan as Jamie took the aniseed balls. Jamie turned towards the door, but rather than going outside, she stopped suddenly.

'Well, speak of the devil,' she said.

2

For a split second, Holly assumed Jamie was joking. Evan had flown to New York on Tuesday, and she wasn't expecting him back until Sunday night. All the travelling he had to do was the worst part of their relationship, but Evan tried to spend his time away in chunks and get as much work as possible done so that the time he spent back in the Cotswolds was focused on them being together, even if that meant he had to spend the day in the sweet shop. In fact, he was now such a common sight behind the till that all the regulars knew him by name, and several of the old ladies seemed terribly disappointed when they showed up and he wasn't working.

But today was Friday. Two days before Evan was due back home and Holly couldn't believe he would have changed plans without telling her. Yet when a tall figure stepped into the shop and leaned down to peck Jamie on the cheek, Holly rushed out from behind the counter, her heart fit to burst.

'What are you doing here? I didn't think you were coming home yet.'

Holly didn't care that this was her workplace, and that there were people around. Reaching up on her tiptoes, she planted her lips against Evan's, and felt a rush of warmth flood through her. A rush of warmth she didn't want to let go of. Eighteen months in, and every time he came back from a work trip away and kissed her like this, it was as though it was their first kiss all over again.

'Well, I was getting a bit lonely,' Evan said. 'Although that's definitely not the case now. And what would you know, I bumped into these guys outside...'

Holly peered behind Evan's shoulder to see an elderly couple, arms laden with shopping bags. From the way Evan had spoken, Holly assumed she was meant to recognise who Evan was with, but these people were entirely unfamiliar.

'Sorry,' she said, confused. 'Do I know you?'

'We just wanted to get into the shop, get some sweets. Is there a reason you're blocking the door?' the man said.

Holly stepped back, horribly embarrassed, and shook her head.

'Oh, I'm sorry. Yes, come in. Come in.'

As the couple walked into the shop, Holly saw who Evan was actually referring to. Her parents, Arthur and Wendy, were standing there, and in their arms, snugly wrapped in a snowflake-patterned all-in-one with her hood over her ears, was Holly's two-year-old daughter, Hope.

'Mummy! Evvy's back,' Hope said, her smile making Holly grin even wider.

'He is back, isn't he? Come here, give Mummy a cuddle. What are you doing here? I thought you were at nursery now?'

'Yes, sorry about that,' Evan said, a look of guilt flashing across his face. 'I picked her up. I checked it was okay with Ben and your parents first, though. I just wanted a chance to see her, and I assumed you'd want to say hello and goodbye, too.'

'Hello and goodbye?' Holly was confused by the statement. In fact, she was confused by a lot of matters. Not only that Evan had turned up early without telling her he was coming, but also that her parents were there. If Evan was the one who'd picked Hope up, it seemed a ridiculous coincidence that they'd all turn up at the sweet shop at exactly the same time.

'I'm sorry, I'm missing something,' Holly said. 'What's going on?'

She looked at Jamie, who had hung around, though her face was as confused as Holly's.

'Well, your dad needed to come down to look after the shop because we want to get going as quickly as possible,' Evan replied.

'Get going?' Holly said, still confused.

'Yes, I've booked us a weekend away. And before you start panicking and tell me how this is the second busiest time of the year for the shop, Caroline and Drey are on board and have sorted out covering your shifts, and Wendy is going to drop Hope with Ben after he finishes work. It's all arranged, but we can check in from three, and it's a four-and-a-half-hour drive, so let's get going, shall we?'

3

Despite Evan's obvious desire to get moving as quickly as possible, Holly still had a few questions. It wasn't that being whisked away wasn't exciting, but it was hard to get her head around it with such short notice. There were logistics to think about. Logistics she was sure Evan hadn't considered.

'I'm sorry. Where are we going?' she asked, hoping that a direct question would get a direct answer.

Unfortunately, Evan wasn't going to fall for that.

'If I told you, it wouldn't be a surprise, would it?' he said. 'But I promise you're going to like it.'

'Okay, but why are we going away right now when, as you pointed out, it's the second busiest time of the year for me?'

Out of the corner of her eye, Holly saw Jamie smirk as she pinched her ring finger. Thankfully, Evan was too busy looking at Holly to notice.

'Because we deserve a weekend away. We've been so caught up with the house, I can't remember the last time you and I actually spent any proper time together relaxing. And we're not going to get a chance to do that with Christmas around the corner and my parents coming to stay. Still, I'd much rather we discussed this on the road than standing in your shop while the traffic gets worse and worse.'

'Fine,' Holly conceded. If there was one thing she knew about Evan, it was that he was determined. If he'd decided they were going on a weekend away together, then that's what they were doing. 'I guess I need to go home and pack my things.'

She had barely finished speaking when her mother stepped forward.

'No, you don't. It's already done,' she said. 'I've packed everything you'll need. Warm clothes, a swimsuit in case there's a hot tub, sensible shoes, and clean underwear.'

She glanced at Holly's father and it was then that Holly noticed the large holdall he was carrying.

'And if there's anything's we've forgotten, we can always buy it,' Evan added.

Holly looked around. The old couple who had come in only a moment ago looked like big spenders and were filling up their arms with boxes of fudge. Most people splashed their cash far more easily at this time of year. Especially when the weather was nice.

At that precise moment, a perfect blue winter sky hung above the frosted fields of the Cotswolds. It was that incredible type of weather that coerced everybody out of the house, as they worried they might not see a clear sky again for several more months. The shop was going to be busy, and even with two of them working, they would be run off their feet. But there was no way Holly could say no to Evan's surprise.

'Well, it looks like you've seen to everything,' she said. 'Which means I'm going to need a very big cuddle from you, Hopey.'

Holly took her daughter from her mother's arms and squeezed her tightly. Giving Hope a cuddle now was a far cry from what it had been when she was a baby. Now, Hope could really squeeze back as she wrapped her arms tightly around Holly's and planted a big kiss on her cheek.

'Miss you, Mummy,' she said, in the way she always did when she was spending a weekend with her dad, rather than Holly and Evan.

'You're going to be a good girl for Daddy and Georgie, right?' Holly asked.

'Hope is always a good girl,' Hope replied sweetly.

'Is that right? Well, I'm going to miss you lots, and I'll send you lots of photos, okay?'

It was the one advantage Holly found in the way her and Ben's relationship had worked out. She never felt guilty about leaving Hope. Ben was a brilliant parent, and Hope was in just as safe hands with him as she was with her. That didn't mean she didn't miss her terribly, though.

'Hope kiss Evvy now?' Hope asked, breaking away from Holly to stretch her arms towards Evan.

Holly could have felt jealous as Hope planted double the number of kisses on Evan's cheeks as she had done for her. The hug lasted a fair bit longer, too, but the sight made Holly's heart swell with disbelief that she shared so much love in her family.

'Well, I guess I should get in there and serve the customers,' her father said, stepping further into the shop. 'And this is for you,' he added, giving Holly the holdall.

'My bag is already in the car,' Evan said, passing Hope over to Holly's mother, planting one last kiss on her cheek. 'It's time we get moving.'

4

They were driving north. That was currently as much as Holly knew. So far, Evan had been less than forthcoming with information about their surprise trip away. He had a bag of similar size to hers in the boot of the car, but there was no suit hanging up, which meant they weren't doing anything formal. Holly was grateful for that. Formal dress required a substantial amount of time to sort out, even though, since being with Evan, she'd had more practice than ever before.

Over the last eighteen months, Evan had taken her to various fancy functions and charity auctions as part of his job. When possible, they turned such events into a weekend away, usually in London, and there was no way Holly would be happy with her mum packing for an evening like that. But they were driving away from the capital, and the fact there was no sign of a suit meant it'd be probably just the two of them this weekend.

'If you won't tell me where we're going, can you at least tell me why we're going away?' she asked. 'You do remember we have a perfectly wonderful house back in Clapton. One that we have spent the last year and a bit renovating?'

'I am well aware of what we've been doing,' Evan said, 'and I already told you, that's the reason we're heading away. We can't have a relaxing weekend at home, even when Ben has Hope, because we always spot something in the house that needs doing: something we haven't bought, something that's not quite straight. It's impossible for you to switch off there, and don't pretend it's not.'

Holly tutted a little, but only because she knew he was right. The house they had bought together was the first ever home that Holly had owned. And it was magnificent. An unexpected inheritance from Maud – which still made Holly's heart throb to think about – combined with Evan's finances too, had enabled them to afford something she would've previously only dreamed about. Five bedrooms, an enormous garden for Holly and Hope to play out in, an office for Evan, and plenty of space for when they expanded their family, too. But Evan was right. All those rooms meant an awful lot of decorating, and even though the main spaces were all sorted, there were still so many things that needed doing. The spare bedroom was at the top of Holly's to-do list. It needed to be done before Evan's family came over for Christmas, but they were having a hard time settling on the colour scheme. Several tins of paint sat in the garage, waiting to be used, but Holly couldn't decide which would be the primary colour and which would be used for the accent wall. Perhaps they would get some inspiration from wherever they were staying. Or perhaps she should just paint it whatever colour she grabbed first and be done with it.

'You see why I wanted to go away?' Evan said. 'And don't tell me you're not thinking about things that need to be done in the house. I know you are.'

Holly let out a resigned sigh. It was wonderful having

someone who knew her as well as Evan did, but it could be a little frustrating, too.

'Okay, so I admit we get a bit distracted with house things. But that doesn't mean we need to go four and a half hours' drive away. There are plenty of perfectly nice places around Bourton in the Cotswolds, like Burford or Bibury.'

'All of which we've been to before on day trips. I want this to be different. I want us to remember this trip.'

Something fluttered in the pit of Holly's stomach as she thought about Jamie pointing to her ring finger. Was this why Evan wanted the trip to be special – because he was going to propose?

She shook her head and hurriedly cast the thought away. There was no way she was going to go into this weekend thinking that; otherwise, she wouldn't be able to enjoy any of the moments they were sharing, fixating too much on when it was going to happen.

'Well,' she said, promising herself she wouldn't think about it again. 'I guess if we've got a four and a half hours' journey to do, I should probably find us some decent music.'

5

An hour and a half into the journey, they stopped for a drink and petrol. At which point, Evan typed the address onto the satnav, and Holly finally knew where they were going.

'Lake Windermere. We're going to the Lake District?' she asked, not bothering to hide her excitement. 'I've never been there. I've never been to the Lake District.'

'I know,' Evan replied.

Holly glanced over her shoulder at the small bag of clothes her mother had packed for her. She hoped there were some jumpers in there. Snow had already fallen on several parts of the UK, including Bourton, but she knew from the news and general geography that the weather was bound to be colder, and possibly snowy too, all that way up north.

'So, we've got a little cottage booked,' Evan said. 'I haven't stayed there myself, but I've had friends who have, and they said the view is amazing. You can see all the way across the lake, and it's close enough that we can walk into town easily, too. My current plan for the weekend is us cosying up on the sofa with a large supply of Christmas films. How does that sound to you?'

'That sounds perfect.'

'And maybe a little walk to the lake, too? You know I miss lakes.'

Almost all the stories Evan had told Holly about his childhood involved trips to the lake, although Holly had proven extremely ignorant about her knowledge of the USA when he told her these stories. She knew he grew up in Washington State, near Seattle, but the only images she'd had of such places were the ones implanted in her mind by films and television shows. It was only when Evan showed her a map of the region that his love of water – and lakes in particular – made sense.

Given how much Evan travelled, he'd been keen for Holly and Hope to visit America and his family over there too, but so far, it just hadn't panned out that way. Last year, his eldest sister had been going through a tricky divorce and they'd decided it was better if he went over alone. Besides, Holly had felt funny about the idea of Hope spending Christmas away from Ben, and so they'd all had a quiet do at Jamie and Fin's.

Still, Holly had met one of Evan's sisters: Ashley. Like Evan, she was the only other one in the family to move abroad, though she still used her parents' place in Seattle as a base while she travelled around working for various charities and NGOs. That summer, she'd had a couple of weeks' vacation, and so they met in the villa in France. She and Holly had got on like a house on fire, with Holly feeling like she had known her for years. Fingers crossed, it would be the same with Evan's parents.

'So now you know where we're going, can you stop fussing about that?' Evan asked. 'And tell me, how is Jamie doing? She looked relaxed at the shop.'

Lately, any conversation that didn't revolve around the house or Hope steered towards Jamie and Fin's impending arrival.

'Has Fin told you if they're having a boy or a girl?' Holly asked, already suspecting she knew the answer.

'No, but I know he's desperate to share it.'

'You know, they won't even discuss names with each other,' Holly said. 'They tried it once, and got into a massive argument, and so now they've made a decision that they're not going to suggest anything until they meet the baby and can agree on what they look like.'

'I don't get that,' Evan said. 'I don't see how some people think that babies look like a certain name. They all look like old men to me. If I was in charge of naming babies based on what I thought they looked like, they'd all have names like Wilfred or Norman.'

Holly chuckled. When Hope was born, she had been, without a doubt, the most beautiful thing she had ever seen in the world, but objectively, yes, there was a chance that she looked like a crinkled old man too.

'I think Jamie's going stir-crazy,' Holly said. 'It might be the shortest maternity leave in history.'

'Well, UK history,' Evan said. 'They don't do maternity leave in the States.'

Holly's jaw dropped. 'What? You're not serious.'

'Let's not get into US politics right now. Anyway, we need to think of a gift. Something amazing. I was thinking a mini quad bike.'

'For a newborn baby?' Holly exclaimed. 'You don't get a newborn baby a quad bike.'

'I know, but we need to make sure that Uncle Evan and Aunty Holly are the most favourite uncle and aunty in the group. There's going to be competition, you know, with Ben, Georgia, Michael, and Caroline, and you know Giles is going to try and cement his position as the favourite uncle too. I can't believe it, that him and

Jamie didn't used to get on. It seems ridiculous given how close they are now.'

Since Holly had moved back to Bourton, Giles's activity had been the most unstable point of stability in her life. There was a time at the beginning of their friendship when she thought they were dating, but then she'd realised he'd actually just wanted to get his hands on her business. Then, it was later on when he was genuinely serious about being with her that Holly became pregnant with Hope, Ben's child. Still, the friendship was quickly healed, unlike Jamie and Giles's, with Jamie refusing to ever let him into her house again. And yet, last year, because of Jamie's wedding, Giles had healed that wound too. They were all a close-knit group, the way she had always hoped they would be, but it was fair to say it had taken a great number of ups and downs to get them to this point.

The closer they got to the Lake District, the more the landscape changed.

'I thought the Cotswolds were hilly,' Holly said as she looked out at the undulating mountains that rose and fell around them. The landscape was unlike anything she had seen or imagined. The earth, barren from the cold months, was, as she'd already suspected, white with snow. As they rose up on the little mountain parts, lakes glimmered beneath them, silvery in the fading light.

'There are some amazing hikes and walks around here,' Evan said, sparking a nervous fluttering in Holly's stomach.

'Hikes? You said we were watching movies, not hiking. I'm not sure I've got the boots for that, not in weather like this.'

Evan laughed. 'Don't worry, the last thing I want is to be responsible for you slipping down and breaking an ankle. But maybe in the summer, if we like this cottage, we could bring Hope back here and do some walks, or we could do them on our own if she's with Ben?'

'That sounds nice.'

Holly was only half listening. Instead, she was gazing out at the scenery, mesmerised by the magnificence of it all. For years, she had been so desperate to travel and see the world, but now she felt like she'd never really appreciated what was on her doorstep.

'I think I'm definitely going to like it here,' Holly said, turning to Evan and flashing him a smile.

'Let's hope so.' He grinned back.

6

Holly was no novice when it came to cute countryside cottages, but the place Evan had picked for them to stay was everything she could have dreamed of and more. While the cottage she had lived in with Hope had been idyllic, with its Cotswold stone walls and enclosed garden, it had been child-friendly. A place made for living full time and, as such, practicality was its main function. This cottage was pure luxury.

'Yep, I'm never going to leave,' Holly said as she dropped onto a large, cream sofa and sank into the deep cushions. There was no way she could have a cream sofa in her house. Not with Hope. But it suited the space here perfectly. Everything suited the space. Wooden beams braced the ceiling, whilst there was an entire wall in the living area that functioned as a bookshelf, filled with beautiful, leather-bound hardbacks. A large sheepskin rug sat on the floor in front of the open fire, and Holly couldn't help but think of some of those romance films she'd seen where an unsuspecting couple, with a strong dislike for each other, got trapped in the snow over the winter, and fell hopelessly in love. Of course, she was already in love.

'So, there's a hot tub outside, and a jacuzzi bath in the en-suite,' Evan said, smiling broadly.

'You're joking?'

'I'm not. I know what my girl likes.'

Evan was right. Holly loved a bath. Baths were her favourite way to while away an evening. But having the choice of a hot tub as well? It was a good job her mother had packed that swimsuit for her. This really was going to be a weekend where she didn't think about work or jobs to do on the house. She was just going to relax.

'I didn't get a food shop done before we left,' Evan said, still standing in the doorway, although Holly was very much in holiday mode as she spread out along the sofa. 'There's a little shop down the road. Why don't I go fetch a few things, and you can have a long bath? Or you can get in the hot tub and wait for me to get back.'

Holly considered the offer. Part of her quite wanted to go for a walk with Evan and see a little more of the area where they were staying, but she knew that this weekend, he wanted to take care of her and there would be plenty of time over the next couple of days to go for a wander.

Still, the hot tub sounded like something she wanted to do with him.

'I'm going to have a bath then,' she said. 'I probably need one, anyway.'

'Wonderful. Well, there should be toiletries and everything there,' Evan said. 'And I'll bring you up a glass of wine when I get back. How does that sound?'

'That sounds like you're the best boyfriend in the world, and I am ridiculously lucky to have you,' Holly said with a grin.

'Well, I'm not going to disagree with that,' Evan replied, kissing her gently. 'I'll be back in a bit. Make yourself at home.'

'Right. I guess we're staying for a couple of nights, so I should probably put the clothes away in the wardrobe.' It was more of a thought that Holly had voiced, rather than a question, but rather than agreeing, Evan reached down and snatched his bag up from by his feet.

'No, absolutely not. You're not to lift a finger. You understand? I'll put these bags in the car if that's what you're going to do.'

'You'll put the bags back in the car?' Holly said, laughing at the comment.

'I mean it. Yup, I'm taking them with me.'

He hoisted both bags onto his shoulder and went to turn around.

'Hold on, I need my wash things out of there.'

Evan frowned. 'Fine, I'll leave yours here, but you're not to do any unpacking, okay? Now, I need to go get some wine before the shop shuts. You know what these local stores are like with closing at crazy-early times. Just make sure you do nothing, okay?'

'You've made it pretty clear that's all I'm allowed to do,' Holly said, before stepping forward and kissing again. 'Perhaps if I'm still in the bath when you get back, you can join me?'

'Sounds perfect.' Evan grinned, before opening the door and heading back to the car, still with his bag on his shoulder.

As Holly ran the oversized tub, she thought about how ridiculous it was. Evan taking his bag with him, just because he didn't want her unpacking anything. But it was when she stepped inside the bath that a sudden thought struck. One so ridiculous, it couldn't possibly be true. What if the reason Evan didn't want her to go through his bag and unpack wasn't because he wanted her to relax, but because there was something in there he didn't want her to see?

Was Jamie right? Was Evan actually going to propose?

7

Holly lay in the bath trying to relax, and yet she couldn't shake the idea from her head. Could that really be why Evan didn't want her to look in his bag? Because there was a ring in there? No, she tried to quash the thought. If he'd bought something as precious and expensive as an engagement ring, he wouldn't just put it in his rucksack and dump it on the floor, would he? Jamie had put ideas into her head, that was all. She was reading too much into things.

Just as Evan had said, there were plenty of luxury bath goodies next to the tub in a wicker basket. Everything from fizzing bath bombs to luxury oils. Having already used a small packet of the bath salts, Holly went to open a bath bomb only to change her mind. Her mum loved things like this. If she left it all unopened, she could take everything back and give it to her as a gift. Besides, it wasn't like the bath wasn't luxury enough, with its bubbling jets and the perfect view from the window, out over the Lake District.

For a few minutes, Holly did nothing but stare. Lazy snowflakes drifted down from the sky. Probably not enough to settle, but enough to once again make her feel like she was the main character in some grand romance novel.

The hot tap continued to run, though Holly's eyes were closed, and she was just drifting off when she heard the door downstairs open.

'So, there wasn't much in the way of food at the shop, but they had wine, and there are a couple of local takeaways,' Evan said as he came up the stairs. He poked his head around the corner, only to grin at the sight of Holly, soaking away in pure bliss. 'Or I could just bring the bottle of wine up here, and we could skip dinner altogether.'

He came across to the bath, leaned over Holly, and planted a long kiss on her lips.

Not once had Holly found a kiss with Evan to be average. Even the pecks on the forehead or quick kisses on the cheek before he went out caused a ripple of warmth to flood through her. She had always thought she'd be worried about having a boyfriend who travelled after the situation with her ex cheating on her, but she hadn't worried about it once with Evan. He was so completely in love with Holly and Hope that she sometimes needed to pinch herself to believe it was real.

As she drew a deep breath in and sat up, Holly's stomach growled loudly. Loud enough to be heard over the bath jets. Evan raised an eyebrow.

'Perhaps we should go for food and an early night?' he said. 'Why don't I grab you the menu for the Indian now? That's the one the woman at the shop recommended. They said there's about a forty-minute wait, so we can ring up now, and then I'll go down and grab it when it's ready, if that sounds okay?'

'That sounds perfect. But I don't have to get out of the bath yet, do I?' Holly asked.

'No,' Evan laughed as he shook his head. 'You don't have to get out of the bath yet.'

When she did finally get out of the bath, Holly intended on

getting dressed in some clean clothes, or perhaps even her night-clothes. Though she hadn't actually checked what her mum had packed. But when she opened up the wardrobe in the bedroom, she found two white, fluffy dressing gowns. The type you found in luxury spas – and the moment Holly ran her hand over the fabric, any thoughts of her own clothes were forgotten. She was going to relax properly this weekend.

By the time she finally came back downstairs into the living room, Evan already had the fire roaring away and was lying on the sofa, reading.

'Food is going to be another ten minutes,' he said, looking up from his book. 'I was going to ask if you wanted to walk down with me, but I guess that's a no.'

'Well, someone has to stay in the house and keep an eye on this fire you've built,' Holly said with a smirk.

'You're very right, of course you do. How responsible of us. But if you want me to get anything else, I'll have to do it now. The weather is getting seriously cold out and according to the woman at the shop, the temperature's going to drop further overnight. I'm not leaving the house again after this.'

'Good, I don't want you to,' Holly said, leaning over to kiss him. When she finally broke away, Holly's gaze shifted past Evan and out of the window. The sun had well and truly set. But the street-lamps were casting the sky in a hazy orange light and the thin dusting of snowflakes continued to flutter down.

'We should probably check the weather forecast. We don't want to get snowed in,' she said.

'Oh, no, that would be the worst thing in the world.'

Evan smirked as he kissed her again before glancing down at his watch.

'I should probably head to the takeaway place now. The pavement was so slippery on the way here, I nearly fell flat on my back. I don't want to be rushing.'

'If you break something, I won't be happy,' Holly said, raising an eyebrow.

'No? I think I'm owed some looking after; remember the way I nursed you with your broken arm? Or have you forgotten about that?'

'We'll see,' Holly said, spying her book on the arm of the chair. Evan must have told her mum to pack it for her.

'Well, I shouldn't be too long. Don't get into any trouble while I'm gone.'

It was only when the front door closed and Holly moved to sit down and grab her book that her eyes fell on the novel Evan had been reading. He must have brought his bag inside and unpacked it. Probably while she was still happily soaking away in the tub.

Holly's chest fluttered at the thought of the bag that he had tried so hard to keep away from her. If there was anything else hiding in it, now was the time to look.

8

Holly was a bad girlfriend. She knew she was. In fact, what she was doing probably went beyond being a bad girlfriend and made her a bad person in general. But her mind wouldn't rest until she knew whether Evan was planning on proposing. She needed to find out if he had brought a ring with him, although what she would do if he had, she wasn't yet sure. Obviously, she would have to pretend she hadn't seen it. That much was common sense, but then what? Would she just act as normal as possible, while secretly spending every minute wondering if this was the moment he was going to do it? What other choice would she have? None. There were no advantages to finding out if Evan had brought a ring with him. She was being ridiculous; Holly knew that, and yet she couldn't stop.

'Two minutes,' she said to herself as she stepped into the bedroom and opened the wardrobe door. 'You can look for two minutes. If you don't find it by then, you have to stop and stop thinking about it, too.'

The strange thing was, until this weekend, Holly really hadn't been that fussed about whether Evan was going to propose. It wasn't like it had been with her first boyfriend, Dan, when getting married had been the ultimate goal. There had been a long list of prerequisites, of course, like buying a house together and making sure they were financially stable. Doing everything 'properly'. Now Holly was eternally grateful that never happened. What had felt like the worst thing she could ever have experienced – Dan cheating on her – had been the catalyst for the most amazing years of her life. As odd as it was, she was grateful to him for it.

But with Evan, life together was an inevitability. It didn't matter if they got married next week, or in ten years' time. It didn't matter if he proposed in some cute, romantic fashion that he'd spent weeks arranging, or whether they simply decided one night, curled up on the sofa, that it was time they took the next step.

Holly knew that she finally had the relationship of her dreams, filled with trust and respect. They were an absolute team. So if that was the case, why was she standing in the wardrobe with her hands in Evan's jeans pocket, wondering if there was a ring inside?

'Pull yourself together – this is ridiculous,' she said aloud.

She removed her hand from the trousers, stepped away, and shut the wardrobe door. She wasn't doing this. She absolutely wasn't doing this.

Determined to do the right thing, she turned around, ready to head back to the living room, when she spotted the handle from Evan's bag poking out from beneath the four-poster bed. Holly paused. It was a strange place to put his bag, wasn't it? There was plenty of room in the bottom of the wardrobe, and there was a beautiful cloakroom downstairs. Why would he have tucked his bag all the way under the bed unless there was something in there he didn't want her to see?

You'll spoil the surprise if you do this. Caroline's voice appeared in Holly's mind, like a little angel on her shoulder, begging her to do the right thing. *He's gone to all this effort to bring you here. To make the moment as romantic as possible. The last thing you want is to ruin that.*

But it won't ruin it. It's just going to make it even more exciting, countered Jamie's voice. *You know he's going to do it. Why is it really such a big deal?*

'It's probably not even in there,' Holly said out loud. 'You're probably making a mountain out of nothing.'

She bit down on her lip, her eyes fixed on the bag. The problem was, now she'd got the idea of a proposal into her head, she was going to be wondering all weekend if it was going to happen. It would probably be better that she checked – just to make sure there wasn't a ring – so that she could get on with enjoying their time away, and not be distracted by such ridiculous thoughts.

A second later, she was pulling the bag out from under the bed and lifting it up onto the mattress.

It was one of those bags that had hundreds of pockets: side pockets, front pockets, internal pockets. Holly went straight to the internal one.

Somehow, she knew. If there was a ring in there, that was where Evan would put it. Zipped securely away.

Before she had time to second guess herself, she plunged her hand into the fabric.

'Oh my God.' She could feel it between her fingers. A small, round box within. 'Oh my God, oh my God, oh my God.'

She bit down again, almost hard enough to draw blood. There was a box in his bag. A ring-sized box. Did she need to know any more than that?

The feel of the item in her hand only made matters worse. Now she was sure there was a ring, but what if there wasn't? What if she'd made a mistake, and it was just an earbud case? Evan was funny about the headphones he went running with. What if he'd got a new pair? That would be the perfect pocket to place them in. If she didn't check, then Holly would spend the entire weekend waiting for a proposal that was never going to happen.

Before she could give herself a chance to change her mind, she pulled the item out of the bag.

The gasp flew from her lips.

There was no mistaking it. Earbuds didn't come in green, velvet boxes with gold gilding. Rings did. Engagement rings.

'You just wanted to check that it was a ring, that's all,' she said to herself. 'You're not allowed to actually look at it.'

She didn't know why she was still talking to herself, perhaps trying to appease her own conscience. Still, she cracked the lid just enough to see that circular rim, only to snap the box closed again.

Holly's heart was pounding in her chest so hard, it was making her breathless, while unusual quantities of sweat beaded on her hands.

This was it. Evan had a ring. He was going to ask her to marry him.

The tiny glimpse had told Holly nothing about the item he was going to use to propose. Which colour was it? She hadn't even been paying enough attention to see properly. Gold, she thought, but she could have got that wrong. Even if she was right, she didn't know what type of stone he'd chosen, and although she was fairly sure it would be a diamond, that didn't tell her much. Was it a solitaire? A trilogy? Something altogether different? The temptation was growing in her again. The desire to just get one proper look. Holly's fingers tightened around the box, ready to lift the lid for a second time, when she heard the key turn in the lock downstairs. A moment later, the front door creaked open.

She scrambled to put the box back in the pocket of the bag, then shoved it all under the bed where it had been before.

'Holly, are you there, babe? I've got food.'

Holly's heart was pounding hard, as if she'd run up a dozen flights of stairs non-stop, and there was even a slight tremble to her knees. Evan was going to propose. She was going to get married.

'Holly?'

'Coming,' she replied, her face unable to control its grin. She needed to give herself a minute. A minute to calm down before she spoke to him, though as she finally gathered herself and headed down to the kitchen, one thought was rolling through her head: when Evan went to sleep that night, she was going to have to text Jamie.

9

'You're very fidgety,' Evan said, as Holly shifted position for at least the fourth time in ten minutes. She had gone from having her head on Evan's shoulder to her head on his lap, but had now switched around entirely and had her feet on his lap instead. That was a position she could normally relax in for hours while they watched a film together. Yet she had barely been lying there for five minutes and already wanted to move again.

'Is everything okay?' Evan asked. 'You're not missing Hope too much, are you?'

'No, it's perfect.' Holly sat upright and adjusting the cushions behind her. 'I guess I'm just finding it harder to relax than I thought I would.'

That was one way of putting it.

Since finding the ring, she'd been unable to relax at all. The nervous energy that had flooded through her while she was searching in the bedroom – a nervous energy she'd thought would stop when she finally found the ring – was now beyond control. It felt like her heart was beating at three times the rate it should and the sense of anticipation meant she'd barely eaten any of the takeaway.

'Well, I thought that tomorrow we could go for a walk down to the lake?' Evan said as he began massaging her feet.

'That sounds lovely,' Holly said truthfully, trying not to think about how perfect a proposal by an ice-covered lake would be.

'And maybe we could get a few Christmas presents while we're at it. There are some lovely shops around here,' Evan carried on. 'We could pick up something a bit different for your mum and dad, and I know my parents love all the quaint things these places sell. I thought we could get a little gift hamper ready for when they come out. You know, filled with all those quintessentially British things, like shortbread and Marmite.'

Holly wasn't sure what she'd think of a hamper with Marmite in, but she loved the idea of collecting a few items to make Evan's parents feel as welcome as possible, although Holly and Evan probably needed to focus on finishing the room his family was staying in before they started thinking about gifts.

The spare bedroom was plastered properly, but there was nothing in the way of fixtures and fittings. The bed was meant to arrive the following week, but until she settled on a colour scheme, it was impossible to buy everything else they needed, like curtains and duvet covers. As much as Holly didn't want to think about it, she was running out of time. In three weeks, his parents were going to be with them.

Normally, Holly spent most of her evenings on the internet, looking for wallpapers and curtain patterns, and colour palettes, but this evening was different. Despite what she told Evan, she couldn't even think about his parents' visit. She was too fixated on the ring.

'I should probably text Ben and Jamie and the others. Let

them know we've got here okay. Do you mind?' she said, hoping that sharing the news might help her stop thinking about it so much.

'You haven't done that already?' Evan said. 'I thought you would have done that when I was out.'

Holly could feel herself turning red. 'I was enjoying a bath, remember?'

'Quite right, and who am I to get in the way of baths?'

He passed Holly her phone, which Holly held on to for a second before deciding whether she was going to send the message she wanted to. She and Evan didn't read each other's phone messages, but it didn't mean they couldn't. She knew the password to his phone, just like he did with hers, but she couldn't imagine he would ever go into it.

'What is going on with your foot? You're really twitchy. Are you sure you're all right? Why don't you FaceTime Ben? Hope might not be asleep; you might be able to chat to her again.'

Holly shook her head. 'I'll be fine,' she said, although in truth, she was going to explode if she didn't tell someone soon.

Opening up her messages, she sent as brief a text as she could to let Jamie know what had happened.

> I found it. You were right.

If she thought that sending Jamie a message about the ring would help her relax and focus on their time in the cottage, Holly was sadly mistaken. Instead, she found herself desperate for a reply, checking her phone every couple of minutes until it finally came through.

Oh my God, oh my God, I knew he had! Message me as soon as he proposes. It's going to be just perfect.

It was such a sweet thing to say, and Holly knew Jamie was right. Whatever Evan had planned, it was bound to be perfect – perfectly simple, perfectly romantic, perfect for them.

Fingers crossed, though, the proposal happened tomorrow, and early on in the day, because Holly wasn't sure how she was going to keep this act up for any longer than that.

10

When Holly woke the next morning, she already had five messages waiting for her from Jamie.

> Has he done it yet?
>
> I told Fin what you found. He already knew! I'm going to divorce him ;-)
>
> Why aren't you responding to any of my messages?
>
> You are gonna tell me first when he does it, right?
>
> Can I tell Caroline? Have you told Caroline? Who's telling Caroline?!

'What are you chuckling at?' Evan asked as he rolled over and kissed her gently on the neck.

Holly quickly threw her phone over towards the side of the bed.

'It was just Jamie,' she said, grateful she could be truthful in that regard. 'She's still struggling to relax.'

'My sister Mel was the same with her last pregnancy. She just wanted to have the baby and get on with the parenting side of things. But then, it was her second.'

Holly thought back to her own pregnancy. That time of her life felt a world away. Everything that had been going on with Ben and Giles had distracted her from just how much her life was going to change when Hope arrived. Still, even if she had thought about it, there was no way she could have imaged her life turning out as incredible as this. And she knew Jamie had just as much of an amazing future ahead of her.

'I keep telling Fin he needs to be ready for Jamie going back to work the day after she gives birth.'

Holly laughed, but she didn't really believe it was true. She had thought much the same about herself, that she would struggle to be away from the sweet shop. But in reality, as soon as Hope arrived, all Holly wanted to do was be with her daughter. Holly had seen often enough how maternal Jamie was with Hope, not to mention Caroline's children. She was one of those women whom children naturally flocked to. She would be an amazing mother.

'I'm hungry,' Holly said, changing the subject as she rolled over, so that she was now facing Evan.

'I'm not surprised. You barely ate anything last night.'

'So where are we going to go? Have you already picked a place?'

Holly wasn't thinking he'd picked a restaurant with the idea of proposing there. It was just that she knew Evan well. It probably came from the fact he travelled so much, but he always researched the best places to eat before they visited anywhere and normally booked a table too, if it was somewhere likely to fill up. She didn't think this weekend away would be any different.

'So, we've got a couple of options,' he said. 'There's a small café in the centre of town that does a great eggs Benedict, according to reviews online, or there's another one right next to the lake.'

'Lake,' Holly said immediately. She knew Evan had picked the Lake District because of how much he loved being by the water. It seemed silly not to take advantage of that. 'Let's go sit by the water.'

'Lake it is,' Evan said. 'Unless you want to stay in bed all morning.'

Holly grinned at him. That was definitely one way to pass the time before the inevitable proposal, but somehow she knew she would be far too twitchy to stay indoors.

'Breakfast and lake first,' she said. 'Then we can come back to bed.'

'Perfect,' he said.

Finally, forcing herself out from under the duvet, Holly went across to the window, where she drew the curtains open.

'Oh wow, there was a lot of snow last night.'

She stared out at the scene in front of her. What had been speckled with white before was now utterly blanketed. Rooftops, trees – there wasn't a hint of colour anywhere.

'I guess we're going to have to wrap up warm for this walk.'

It took another forty minutes to get them out of the house. Holly decided layers were the way forward, and ended up putting on half the clothes her mother had packed for her, and even when she was fully dressed, she remained dubious as to whether she would be warm enough.

'How come Mum always overpacks for herself and barely packed anything for me?' she asked, although thinking about her mother caused another thought to rise to the top of her mind. Did her parents know? Had Evan already told them that he'd bought a ring? It seemed likely. Despite how quickly their relationship had moved forward initially, Holly knew how old-fashioned Evan was.

He would want to do things properly. He had almost certainly told her father he was planning a proposal. He wouldn't have asked his permission, though. That was something different. Holly didn't need her parents' permission to marry the person she loved, and Evan knew that. But the more she thought about it, the more she was sure Evan would have spoken to them. Were they sitting at home, waiting for the moment Holly rang to let them know?

Determined to not think about it any longer, she said, 'Okay, I've got my winter boots. I've got my gloves. I've got my scarf.'

She checked her pocket for her wallet and phone before making sure they were zipped in securely. If the moment happened today, she definitely wanted to take some photos immediately afterwards.

'Great,' Evan said. 'Then let's see what these lakes are all about up close, shall we?'

11

Holly struggled to imagine a more perfect scene. The sky was a palette of blues, streaked with feather-like clouds, while the lake itself was a far darker reflection. The surface looked somewhat unusual, not least because there were dozens of seagulls standing on top of it. Not swimming in it, but standing on top.

'I can't believe a lake this size would freeze,' Holly said, looking out at the giant mass of frozen water. 'It's crazy.'

'If this was in the States, or Canada, you know that people would be ice-skating on it. Ice-skating on lakes, there's nothing quite like it.'

'I think the ice has to be a fair bit thicker for that, doesn't it?'

'Probably. Temperatures have been freezing here for a while now, though. I bet if you go back fifty years, you'd have the whole town out here.'

Holly shook her head and shuddered at the thought. That was like those crazy people who did cold-water swimming. What pleasure could possibly be garnered from dipping yourself into freezing-cold water and watching your limbs turn blue? And as for the health benefits, well, she'd rather cut down on a couple of her sweets than plunge herself into an icy abyss at regular intervals.

She snuggled up closer to Evan, trying to get warmer.

'Do you know what? I think I might be ready for that breakfast,' she said. 'Maybe it'll warm me up a bit, and afterwards, we can feed the ducks.' She pointed to a small group of birds sitting on the lakeside. Unlike the seagulls, they at least had the common sense to stay off the ice, although they didn't look very happy. 'We'll see if we can get some bread in the café. I'm sure they won't mind selling us a couple of pieces.'

She turned back, ready to walk up towards the café, when she noticed Evan was still standing in the same spot, not moving.

'Evan? What is it?'

Holly's pulse soared as, for a split second, she thought that this was the moment. He was going to call her back to him, so that he could drop down on one knee and propose, but a moment later, she realised that wasn't the case. He was staring intently off into the distance.

'There are some kids there, playing by the ice,' he said. 'I don't like the look of it.'

Holly stepped forward. She quickly saw who Evan meant. It was a group of three lads. Two were standing on the shoreline, while the other was edging further out, almost undoubtedly goaded by his friends.

'I'm sure the locals know what they're doing. They probably do this every year,' Holly said, sounding reasonable to herself, but Evan was shaking his head.

'It doesn't freeze every year. The lakes here don't freeze that often at all. No, that's a disaster waiting to happen.' Without even a glance towards Holly, Evan started walking towards them. 'I've got a bad feeling about this,' he said, his stride getting longer and longer, and faster and faster, until he was practically sprinting.

'You need to get back,' he yelled at the boy. 'The ice gets thinner the further out you go. You need to get back.'

The two lads on the shoreline looked at him fleetingly, but the one out on the ice was still moving.

'The ice gets thinner. You need to get back!' Evan yelled again, but they weren't looking any more.

Holly was now having to sprint to keep up with Evan, who was going full pace, when he finally reached the two boys.

'What the hell is he doing out there?' Evan snapped. 'Any second, he's going to fall in; he's not a bloody seagull.'

Only a moment ago, Holly had been confident the other boys were goading the one on the ice, but now she wasn't so sure. Their faces were near white.

'We know, we told him. We just said to step on the edge. That's all. But he won't stop. I don't think he can hear us.'

'He can hear you,' Evan said. 'The ice is gonna break!' he yelled. 'The ice is going to—'

He didn't get to finish his last sentence. That was the moment the ice shattered, and the boy plunged into the water.

12

'Oh, God. Oh, God.'

The boys on the shore didn't know what to do or where to look, and neither did Holly. One second, the lad had been out there, standing on the ice; a second later, he was gone. His arms appeared out of the water as he flailed about, but that was all she could see.

'We need to help him; we need to do something,' Holly said, only to realise that while she was panicking, Evan was already acting.

He had stripped off his coat and jumper and was already one step onto the ice.

'I'm calling an ambulance!' Holly yelled as she grabbed her phone out of her pocket, only to hear the boys talking beside her.

'Yes, ambulance. We need it fast. Please. Please come fast,' one of them said.

Knowing that the ambulance was on its way, Holly turned her attention back to the lake. Evan was running across the ice now and she could see it cracking beneath his feet. He wasn't as light as the boy, nowhere near, and Evan's feet were hammering on the ice with such force that it was cracking beneath him. Would he make it? He had to.

A second later, he plunged into the water after the boy.

'Evan!' Holly dropped to her knees, so shocked she could barely breathe.

'Yes, they're in the ice. Two of them. I didn't know he was going to do it. I didn't know he was going to do it.'

Holly could hear the boys still talking to the emergency services and knew she should take control. She was the adult in the situation. She was the one who should be able to act calmly, but Evan had just plunged himself into icy water after a boy he didn't know. Someone who had gone in behaving completely irresponsibly.

'Please, please, please let them be all right.'

She was still speaking aloud when she saw the pair of them reach the surface. Evan had the boy over his shoulder and was dragging him back towards the shore, cracking the ice with his body as he fought to get there.

'Break the ice, break the ice for them!' Holly shouted, finally seeing something she could do to help. She stepped forward onto the shallower ice, and smashed her feet hard on the surface, causing it to shatter out. The sudden cold made her shock even greater, and it was only up to her calves. She could only imagine how cold Evan and the boy were.

The boys were both were doing what she'd said, helping her crack the ice. 'Please don't let him be dead,' one was muttering.

Somehow, Evan was still moving, still swimming towards the shore. He was still going; he was still okay.

Holly waded in until the water was up to her hips.

'Grab him!' Evan gasped. 'Grab him, get the kid's jumper off, put a coat around him.'

His voice was high-pitched, and it didn't sound like Evan, but

Holly barely had time to think about that. She was looking at the boy. His pale face was ashen, and it was impossible to tell if he was even breathing.

'Quickly,' Evan urged.

'Give me a hand,' Holly said, calling out to the boys. Together, she and one of the other lads grabbed the boy and dragged him towards the surface.

The moment he was on the grass, Holly started unzipping his top.

'What are you doing?' the boy said, pushing her away.

'It's freezing. His top is like ice. You need to get a dry top on him. Something to warm him up.'

The boy hesitated for a moment before following Holly's lead and stripping off his own coat.

As he did so, Holly looked back to the water, where Evan had pulled himself right onto the shoreline and was there, hugging his knees.

'Get something dry on him,' she repeated before racing over to Evan. 'What the hell did you do that for?' she said, dropping down beside him. 'You could've died. You could've died.'

'I'm okay, I'm okay,' Evan replied, his voice quiet and cracking. 'The boy? What about the boy?'

'They're getting him dry. It's you I need to worry about,' Holly said, only now realising that while Evan had given them advice to help the boy, he had completely ignored it himself. He was still dripping wet and freezing and shaking so much, she could hardly get a hold of his top. 'Lift your arms up; let me take your top off. It's okay. Please, Evan. I just need to get this one off you, then you can have my coat; you can have my coat.'

'The boy, he's going to be okay though, isn't he?' Evan was saying. It was all he was repeating.

'Please, I need to do this for you,' Holly insisted. 'He's fine, the boy's fine. We need to get you dry. We need to get you dry and warm.'

Somehow, even through the shaking, Holly managed to slip the sodden arms off from Evan's top. The entire thing was crisp to the touch, as if it was already freezing and it felt like forever before she finally yanked the rest of it off over his head and put her own coat over his bare shoulders instead. She was just doing up the zip when one of the boys yelled.

'The ambulance is here!'

Holly turned towards them to see the flashing lights approaching.

'I'm going to tell them what happened. I'll be one minute, okay?' she said to Evan. 'I'll be one minute.'

She raced up to the ambulance, where a paramedic was leaping out of the van.

'Is there anyone in the ice?' they asked. 'Anyone in the water?'

Holly shook her head. 'My boyfriend went in after the boy. They're both out now, but please, they were in there a while. They're so cold.'

'It's fine, it's fine. We'll look after your boyfriend. He's down there?' The man nodded towards the lake.

'Yes, he's shaking. He's shaking so much,' Holly said. 'But he's still speaking. That's good, isn't it? He'll be okay, right? He's speaking, so he'll be okay?'

'We're here now. We'll take control of the situation.'

The other paramedic had already gone straight to the boy, while the first one opened the back of the van.

'Go back to your boyfriend,' the paramedic said. 'Keep him talking; I'll be there in one second.'

Holly nodded repeatedly, a sense of relief adding some warmth to her body. The paramedics were here; it was going to be all right now.

She sprinted back down to Evan.

'It's okay, they're here, you're going to be all right,' she said. 'Did you hear? The paramedics are here, okay?'

She rested her hand on Evan's shoulder and spoke again, but he didn't so much as tilt his head towards her. His body was flopped forward. He wasn't shaking any more.

13

Another ambulance had arrived, and the boy was already being lifted into the first. It was a moment longer before two paramedics appeared at Holly's side and hoisted Evan onto a gurney.

'Please tell me he's going to be okay,' Holly said as she climbed into the ambulance after him, not even asking if that was something she was allowed to do. If it wasn't, they would have to drag her out kicking and screaming. She wasn't going to leave Evan's side.

A moment later, and the sirens were on as the ambulance raced away down the road.

Holly stared at Evan in disbelief. Ice crystals glistened in his wet hair, and his lips were tinged blue; he barely looked alive.

'He's going to be okay, isn't he? He was talking before. Why's he stopped? Why isn't he talking now?'

Holly knew her talking wasn't helping the paramedic do his job. She knew she needed to step back and let him work, but he didn't seem to be doing anything other than monitoring and whispering things into his radio. The ambulance felt as if it had only started driving and yet it was slowing again. Why were they slowing down? she wanted to ask. Were the cars moving out of their way? Why weren't they driving faster and what was the point of all these machines and equipment if the paramedic wasn't going to use them? Holly wanted to scream with all the questions that filled her head. Questions she knew it wouldn't help to ask. Yet, as if knowing what she was thinking, the paramedic reached up and grabbed a medical device that Holly recognised immediately. A defibrillator.

'No,' she said. 'His heart? Has his heart stopped? It can't have.'

'I just need to give it a bit of a hand, that's all,' the paramedic said. 'Get it back to a regular rhythm. Just mind out of the way. You need to let go of his hand now.'

Holly looked down. She hadn't even realised she'd been holding on to Evan, but her knuckles were white from how hard she'd been gripping him.

'You need to let go of him, please,' the paramedic said again.

This time, she listened.

Holly didn't want to watch and yet she couldn't tear her eyes away as the paramedic stuck the pads to Evan's bare chest. A second later, a high-pitched tone filled the ambulance. She watched as the man sent the shock through Evan's body, but there was no great jerk of his chest, the way she always saw in Hollywood movies. Why was that? Had it not worked properly? Had he not needed it?

'He went in to save the boy? Is that right?' the paramedic said.

'Yes. He went in after him. He wasn't in the water as long. Evan was swimming, though. He didn't slip. He was dragging the boy back to the shore. He had to break the ice; he had to break the ice to get him back.'

The image was playing over and over in Holly's head. Evan

disappearing into the ice then reappearing only a second later with the boy in his grip. Why had she stood on the shore and watched them for so long? Why hadn't she gone in deeper and got him out sooner?

The paramedic nodded sympathetically as he set the defibrillator for a second time. Holly wanted to ask what he was doing and why the first one hadn't been enough, but her throat was blocked again. Clogged with tears she wouldn't let fall. She couldn't help Evan if she was a blubbering mess.

'Brave guy,' the paramedic said.

Holly waited for him to add more. Something about how it would only be a few minutes until Evan's body was warmed up again. Until he was talking to her and apologising for the biggest scare of his life, but there was nothing.

'Is your boyfriend a swimmer?' the paramedic said instead. 'Did he go swimming places like this before? He knew to take his coat off and things?'

Holly's eyes remained locked on Evan and the machine that was still fixed to his chest. Why was the paramedic asking about whether Evan swam? It didn't make sense, but then, she thought, he probably wouldn't have asked her if it didn't matter.

'He's American. He grew up by Seattle. There are lots of lakes there. He did a lot of swimming as a child there. And he has a villa in France too. He goes swimming there a lot. In the pool, though.'

'Right, good, good.' The paramedic paused, then looked at Holly. 'All right, we're at the hospital. There are doctors here waiting. We need to make sure they've got room to get to him. So just stay where you are for a second so I can get him out, okay? It'll just be a minute.'

Holly nodded, but she was only half listening. They were at the hospital. That was what mattered. There were at the hospital and the doctors would see to Evan.

The ambulance drew to a stop, and Holly grabbed onto Evan's hand, wanting to hold him for just a second longer, but her skin had barely touched his when the back doors swung open.

'Let's get moving, people!' someone said.

14

It was like a scene from a medical drama. The instant the back door swung open, doctors were there on hand to pull Evan from the vehicle, while speaking with words Holly barely understood.

Only when she knew he was safely in their hands, did Holly step out of the ambulance.

'Thank God. Thank God you're okay.'

Holly looked to the side to the person who'd spoken, and it was then she saw the other ambulance had arrived moments before them. The two boys who had stayed on the lakeside were there with their parents. The third was on a gurney, rolling into the hospital, although Holly could see the tinge of colour that had returned to his cheeks.

'I'm sorry,' the boy stuttered to the man walking beside him as he tried to sit up. 'I'm sorry. Will you find out about the other guy? The one who went in after me? Will you find out if he's okay?'

Holly stared at the boy as he was guided away from her. He was speaking. He was speaking to people. How could he do that when Evan couldn't? Had he needed a defibrillator, too? Perhaps Evan would start speaking in a minute, she thought. Perhaps he was already talking to the doctors, telling them what had happened.

Holly's legs didn't feel like her own as she followed the doctors in through the double doors towards the hospital. The lads, who must've been around fifteen, collapsed into their parents' arms and sobbed, as if they were no older than Hope. As she watched on, Holly found herself desperate to do the same. She wanted somebody's arms to collapse into, but there was no one there for her.

'You came in with the man at the lake, didn't you?' a doctor asked, causing Holly to stop in her tracks.

'Yes... Yes, I did. Is he going to be okay? When will I be able to speak to him?'

'If you wait here, we'll let you know as soon as we've got some news,' she said, gently touching Holly's arm. 'Just take a seat.'

'Please, please, just tell me when I can see him?' Holly said. 'Can I come with him? I don't want to be away from him. Please.'

The doctor pressed her lips together, yet before she said anything, she glanced behind her to where another doctor was standing and staring straight at them.

'I'll just be a moment,' the first doctor said, before turning around and walking towards them.

Holly's attention remained locked on the two doctors, although from what she could tell, they weren't actually saying anything. They simply exchanged a look before the first one turned around and came straight back to Holly.

'If you want to come with me,' she said.

'To see Evan?' Holly replied, but the doctor didn't answer, and so Holly followed her, past the reception, and into a small room with pulled-down blinds and several soft chairs.

'Will you bring him here?' Holly said. 'I really just want to be with him. I won't get in your way. I promise.'

The doctor's lips parted, and she drew a long inhalation through her nose.

'I'm so sorry. I'm afraid there was nothing we could do.'

'What do you mean?' Holly asked.

'I'm ever so sorry. I mean, he's gone. Your husband didn't make it.'

15

Holly was sitting on one of the grey cushioned chairs, but she couldn't remember sitting down. She couldn't remember moving at all. Someone had given her some forms to fill in with her name and Evan's details, but she couldn't remember who had done that either. All she knew was that she was waiting for a doctor to come and talk to her. She remembered that part. She was waiting for a doctor, but what good would they do now?

Your husband has died. Those were the words that were said to her. 'Your husband has died.' But she didn't have a husband. She didn't even have a fiancé yet. That was meant to have happened, though. This weekend, Evan was going to propose to her. Then they would get married. Then she would have a husband. Her mind felt like it was wading through a fog, all the thoughts that formed in it blurred or obscured. The doctor must have been confused. Misunderstood the situation. So perhaps she was wrong about what had happened. It wouldn't be the first time, right? You heard about those situations on the news where people's heartbeats went so low, they looked as if they had died, but they hadn't.

It was possible, wasn't it? Or maybe the doctor had spoken to the wrong person. Yes, that made sense. That was why she had said husband and not boyfriend: because it wasn't Holly she had meant to talk to. There was some other woman. Some other woman who was already married to the love of their life, sitting in the waiting room, who didn't know that they had already lost them. That had to be the case, didn't it? Because Evan couldn't be gone. He just couldn't.

Holly was staring into nothing when the door opened.

The doctor who walked in looked younger than Holly. Her red hair was neatly plaited down the side of her shoulder. She came in slowly, shutting the door all the way again, before she took a seat opposite Holly.

'Mrs Berry?'

'Miss,' Holly corrected. 'Miss Berry. I'm not married. We're not married yet.'

The doctor nodded slowly.

'I hear your partner— Your boyfriend,' she corrected herself, clearly not sure what the correct word to use in the situation was. 'I hear he raced into the water to save a young man's life.'

Holly nodded. 'He did. The boy, is he... Did he...?'

A small smile curled at the corner of the woman's lips.

'He's got a long road of recovery ahead of him,' she said. 'Being in the water that length of time has its effects, but he will be okay.'

A slight, stifled gasp left Holly's lips as she felt the tears rolling down her cheeks.

'And Evan? Evan, is he...?'

'I'm so sorry,' the doctor said. The smile was gone and her eyes looked glazed. 'Is there someone you can call? You're not from around this area, are you?'

Holly shook her head. 'I don't understand, though. He was in the water for less time. And he's healthy, he's so fit. He runs every morning at five-thirty, even in the winter. I don't understand.'

'I know.' The doctor was leaning forward, her hands clasped on the folder as she spoke. 'The onset of hypothermia, which is what caused your husband's rapid deterioration—'

'He's not my husband,' Holly snapped.

The doctor's cheeks coloured. 'I'm sorry, yes. Sorry. Your boyfriend, I should have said. I'm sorry. The onset of hypothermia is what caused your boyfriend's body to shut down, and it can come on very quickly if the body is under more stress. I heard he was the one swimming back to the shore with the boy, dragging him, breaking the ice, in fact.'

'We broke some of it for him, too. To make it easier.'

Holly wasn't sure why she said such a thing. It sounded ridiculous. Maybe she just wanted the doctor to know that she'd tried to make it easier for Evan. That she hadn't done nothing at all. That she hadn't just let him go out there.

'So, that's it. He's just gone?'

'I can't imagine what this must be like for you,' the doctor said, her voice heavy with sympathy. 'We have people here on site to support you.'

'He was going to propose,' Holly said, her voice barely a whisper. 'I found a ring. That's what this weekend was for. He wasn't meant to leave me. He wasn't meant to leave me like this... How could this have happened?'

'I'm sorry. I'm so sorry for your loss.'

Holly didn't know how long the doctor stayed there, wordlessly holding Holly's hand. No doubt she had more important places to be and countless lives to save. But instead, she stayed there with Holly, trying to ease her pain. Not that anything could. Evan was gone; he was actually gone.

When the doctor finally broke away, her expression was solemn. 'I'm sorry, I will have to go now. But you can use this room, okay? You can stay here, and nobody is going to disturb you. Do you have somebody you can ring? Somebody who can come and get you? Or would you rather us ring someone?'

Holly looked up at the doctor, but it was only after an extended pause that she realised she was expected to answer.

'Yes, yes, I do.'

When the doctor left, Holly sat there in silence. How could life change so quickly? Instantly, even. One minute, she had been on top of the world, and now? Now she was on her own. One minute, she had been thinking only of the future and all the incredible adventures that awaited her. Now that future was gone and all the plans she'd made were worthless, all the dreams she'd formed as ephemeral as storm clouds.

It was impossible to know how much time passed before Holly picked up her phone. There was a clock on the wall, and she could hear the seconds ticking by on it, but they didn't mean anything to her. The passing of time meant nothing now.

Holly wasn't really thinking about who she should tell first about Evan. All she was thinking was that she had to tell someone. And so she mindlessly scrolled down her contacts list, found a name, and called them.

The phone was answered in one ring.

'Oh my God, is he there? Did it happen?'

For a split second, Holly didn't understand why Jamie sounded so excited. So happy. 'Did it happen?' What did she mean by that? But then the memory of why she was meant to be ringing her friend returned, daggers in her heart.

'Holly, come on, I want the details. I need to know everything.'

'Yes, everything. You need to know everything,' Holly repeated.

It was true. At some point, she would need to tell them every last detail, about the boy and the rescue and how she wished she had broken more of the ice. But at that moment, there was only one thing she could say.

'Evan has gone, Jamie. He's died. Evan is dead.'

16

It was only after Holly had hung up the phone that she realised what she had done. How selfish and unthoughtful she had been. She could've rung her parents, she could have rung Ben, or Fin, or Caroline, but she had chosen Jamie because she wanted to hear Jamie's voice. Jamie who had expected Holly to be ringing with incredible news, but worse still, was pregnant. Holly knew that stress had an effect on babies, and she had thoughtlessly and self-ishly placed all that on her.

'No, no. I don't understand?' Jamie's disbelief mirrored Holly's own. The agony in her words multiplying the pain Holly felt. 'You don't mean it. You can't. He can't be.'

'Holly, what is it? What's going on?' Fin had taken over the telephone call, and Holly knew he'd expect her to say those words again, but she couldn't. Her throat had closed shut, as if it was refusing to say them.

'A boy fell in the ice. Evan saved him.'

That was all she could manage.

'And he...' The rest of Fin's words faded into nothing and when he spoke again, the emotion was gone and in its place was a far more organised tone. 'All right,' he said. 'One of us will get to you as soon as we can. I'll just see who's closest. I know Michael is doing some work; he might be a bit nearer. Just... it will be okay. One of us will come and help you. You won't be alone. We're here. If you want to keep talking, we're here, okay?'

Holly nodded and hung up the phone without another word.

So that was it. She was just supposed to wait in the hospital for someone to come and help her deal with whatever came next. But what did come next? She'd not been through this before, not with her parents, not with anybody. The thought of her parents caused another crack to break open in her chest. She would need to ring Evan's mum and dad. She had spoken to them earlier in the week and they had talked about how excited they were to be visiting for the first time. Now they had lost their only son, their youngest child, and she would need to be the one to tell them how.

The thought was immediately countered by another, as Holly considered how perhaps Fin was already doing it now. It made sense if he was the one who broke the news. After all, he'd known them for decades. Either way, it brought her little relief; Holly would still need to speak to them at some point. They, like everyone else, would need to know what happened, and she would have to tell people again and again and again.

And what about Hope? How would she explain to Hope that the man she loved almost as much as her own father wasn't coming back? That he had gone? How could she explain that to her?

The air rushed from Holly's lungs as she struggled to breathe. Could she really break her own daughter's heart like that? She knew how sensitive Hope was. She wouldn't understand; she would think she had done something.

It was shortly after the phone call when a nurse came in and told Holly she would take her to see Evan. If that was what she wanted. Holly wasn't sure if she answered or not. It was as if there was a delay between her mind and her body. Or rather, a detachment. Thoughts no longer seemed linear, and it felt as if the nurse had only just posed the question when Holly was there, in another part of the hospital, looking at Evan on the metal bed, the white sheet pulled over his chest.

'I'll just wait outside until you're ready for me to take you back to the waiting area,' the nurse had said before leaving Holly alone with Evan. Only it wasn't Evan. It couldn't be.

Holly's heart drummed in her chest as she reached out to touch his hand, only to find it icy cold. She jerked back away from him. This wasn't right. She wasn't meant to see him like this. She didn't want to see him like this. Swallowing back the tears, she spun around and rushed out into the corridor to where the nurse was standing, flicking through her phone.

'I'm done,' Holly said. 'Take me back. Take me back now.'

'You're done already?' The nurse didn't hide the surprise in her voice. 'Don't you want some more time? People normally want more time.'

'Just take me back to the waiting room,' Holly snapped.

Unlike before, the nurse didn't object.

Once again, Holly's body and mind detached, and before she knew it, she was back in the grey chair, with nothing to do but wait.

Normally, when she had spare time like this, she would flick through her phone, looking for things for the house. But what happened to the house now? How would that work? It was far too big for her and Hope alone. There was no need for the spare bedrooms, for the extra children, or Evan's office that he worked in when he wasn't travelling. There was no need for so many parts of their life if Evan wasn't in it. And so, in that same grey chair where the doctor had sat beside her, Holly remained, consumed by the enormity of her grief.

Holly wasn't sure where the urge to move came from. She thought that perhaps the doctors might need the room for somebody else to tell them that the person they loved most in the world was gone. And while time didn't move quite the same way as it had before, the clock on the wall showed several hours had passed.

She didn't know which of her friends was going to come and meet her, but after travelling all this way, she wanted to make their life as easy as possible, and her hiding away in some hidden room with the blinds down wouldn't make her easy to find. So she moved to the waiting area.

For a second, she observed the people with a sense of detachment. There were children holding their parents' hands and adults coughing in handkerchiefs or with masks over their faces. Did they know that in a second, their lives could be torn apart and everything they knew could be snatched from them in a heartbeat? She looked at a small child of a similar age to Hope. In his hand was a large, grey bunny, almost identical in style to those Evan had given Hope when they first met. Holly's breath lurched, and she turned away before taking a seat at the very edge of the waiting room, facing out towards the window.

Given the time it took to travel from Bourton, Holly had expected to be sitting there until late afternoon. Perhaps even to the evening, but a voice said her name.

'Holly?'

Holly had expected to notice when someone showed up for her, but her thoughts had made it difficult for her to see anything. Still, when she lifted her head, Giles was there, standing right in front of her.

'I am so sorry,' he said again, his voice quiet. 'Evan has really gone.'

17

Holly didn't recall much about the hours that followed that day. Like the ins and outs of the hospital paperwork or the journey back from the Lake District to Bourton. She didn't remember much of what happened the following day either. But what she did recall was Fin telling her that Evan's mother was flying over from the States to help with the arrangements, and so now, two days after Evan's death, Holly was sitting in the car, gripping the steering wheel and staring at the glass jars of sweets in the window of Just One More, while Hope gabbled away in the back seat.

Her plan wasn't to simply sit outside the sweet shop. She needed to get out of the car and go inside. She was going to go inside. She just needed a minute first. Somehow, going into the sweet shop felt like the hardest thing of all, and Holly had done a lot of hard things over the last two days.

Thankfully, Giles had sorted everything in the Lake District, from arranging someone to collect Evan's car and packing up their things in the cottage, to dealing with all the hospital administration, which involved collecting Evan's belongings. Belongings that included the solitaire diamond ring, which now sat on Holly's ring finger and had done since the moment Giles handed it to her. No one had said anything about Holly wearing it, even though everyone knew Evan hadn't had a chance to propose. But then, people hadn't said that much to her at all, except how sorry they were.

Holly's parents had been waiting at her house when she arrived home late on Saturday evening. They had run her a bath she didn't want to soak in and fixed her food she had no desire to eat. Then they had offered to stay the night with her, as had Giles, but Holly had sent them all away. She didn't need people. She needed to get on with things. Like cleaning the kitchen and the bathrooms and making sure the house was presentable for when Evan's mother came.

'How are you going to tell Hope?' Her mother had said to Holly as she reappeared on Sunday morning with pastries and fruit, under the guise of bringing breakfast. 'Have you thought about what you're going to tell her?'

Holly had tried to swallow the lump that had been filling her throat since the hospital, although she already knew that was impossible. It was like her body had changed. Reacted to the fact that Evan was no longer there in her life. It didn't want food any more, and no matter how tired she felt, she couldn't fall asleep at night, although when morning came around, her eyes felt so heavy, she could barely keep them open. But being around Hope was the one thing that made her feel normal. That made her feel like she still had a reason to get up each day and be the best person she could.

'I'll tell her when the time feels right,' Holly had said to her mother, and that was what she had planned. Only so far, that right moment hadn't yet appeared. Holly and Hope had spent the whole day on Sunday, baking and drawing, and Hope had asked where Evvy was over a dozen times. But she had been so happy, singing and laughing as she cracked eggs into the mixing bowl and spooned cake batter into tins and Holly had just wanted to hold on to that happiness for a little longer. And by the time Monday morning rolled around, Holly had more immediate things to deal with. Like the fact that Evan's mother, Anne, had flown in from America and after years of chatting on video calls, Holly was finally going to meet her face to face. The last thing she wanted was to turn up unprepared and empty-handed.

With a sudden burst of momentum, Holly pushed the car door open, swung her legs outside and stood up. She barely had her feet on the tarmac when a voice said her name.

'Holly? What are you doing here?' Caroline said, stepping out of the shop and onto the pavement next to Holly. 'I thought you were going to see Evan's mum this morning. She's already landed, right?'

Holly wasn't surprised Caroline knew Anne was coming. That was the way they were: constantly sharing information between one another. It wasn't gossip. Holly hadn't understood that at first – this village mentality. This desire to know everything that was going on in everyone's lives wasn't just a case of insidious gossip. Of course, there were one or two bad eggs in every clutch, but in most cases, people in the village just cared. That was definitely the case with Caroline, who Holly had known longer than any other of her friends in Bourton. Yet the manner in which Caroline looked at her, with her eyes full of pity, made her want to curl into herself.

'Yes. I just came in to get some sweets.'

'Sweets?' Caroline said, a slight frown crumpling her brow. 'I can get you those. What do you want? I can bring them to you. Just tell me what it is you're after. I'll drop them at your place when I've shut up here. Or I can drop them at Fin's if that's easier?'

'It's fine, I can do it. I just want to get a few things. You know. For Anne. So that she can take them back to the others if she wants to.'

Holly wasn't sure what she was saying. She didn't know how long Anne would be staying for, or if she even had any luggage room to take things with her. Of course, there was nothing to have stopped her arriving with a dozen empty suitcases, ready to pack all Evan's belongings into, so that she could take them back to his family home and away from Holly. But Holly couldn't think about that. Now that she had mentioned getting sweets to take to Anne, it seemed like a sensible thing to do. Even if Anne didn't want them, she was sure there would be someone back in the States who would enjoy them.

Holly's jaw clenched as she thought about the hamper she and Evan had discussed making for his parents when they came over. Had they talked about that the day he died, or was it the day before? she thought, her pulse kicking up a notch. She knew they'd talked about it before the weekend as she'd looked online for a large wicker basket to put all the items in, but had she and Evan had discussed it? It was Saturday, wasn't it? Holly's pulse was drumming now, causing a hammering behind her temples. Had that been the last conversation they'd had before he'd dived into the water?

As she stood on the pavement with her mind racing away, she realised she couldn't remember. She couldn't remember what she and Evan had last spoken about. She remembered what Evan said about the boy and putting the dry clothes on him after he'd dragged him out of the water. But what about before they'd noticed him on the ice? What was the last conversation Holly had had with Evan before he left her?

The tightness around Holly's chest clamped harder and harder, as she struggled to breathe.

'Holly? Are you okay?' Do you need to sit down? I can get Hope?

Hope. Her daughter's name was all it took to bring Holly back to the present. *Where was she?* Holly's pulse hammered so hard behind her ears, she felt as if her head was underwater. *Where was Hope?* she thought again.

In a near-blind panic, Holly spun around to see her daughter staring at her through the window. A gasp flew from Holly's lips. Hope was there. She was fine.

'Holly?' Caroline said again. A heat filled the crisp winter air as Holly's eyes moved between Caroline, Hope, the shop and back again. Her pulse was going back down now. Her breathing still shallow, but steadier. Hope was fine. Holly needed to focus on that. She needed to focus only on what she could control, and that was making sure her daughter was as loved and happy as possible. But she couldn't be there standing outside the shop. Not with Evan's memory hanging in the doorway.

'Do you know what?' Holly said, straightening herself up and coaxing her lips to make something that resembled a smile. 'I think you're right. I think I should go straight to see Anne. Could you put together a hamper for me and get Dad to drop it over at Fin and Jamie's when he comes in?'

'Of course,' Caroline said, though a deep frown remained etched between her brows. 'Holly, you know we're here, right? We're all here for you if you need us.'

Holly forced a smile onto her face. One so tight, it made her cheeks ache.

'Of course, but you don't need to worry about me. I'm fine. Honestly, I'm really fine. I just want a nice hamper of sweets for Anne. That's all.' A moment later, Holly was climbing back into the car and driving away.

18

Holly didn't go straight to Fin and Jamie's. Instead, she drove up to Stow and took Hope in a trolley around the supermarket. Holly wasn't sure what they needed, exactly. She hadn't even checked the fridge when she left – there were more than enough cakes and muffins to keep Hope going – but Holly had filled the trolley, anyway. Mindlessly adding fruit and vegetables and not even thinking about what she was going to cook with them. Afterwards, Holly took Hope to a café for lunch.

'This is nice, isn't it, Hopey?' Holly said, as she cut up pieces of her jacket potato and placed them on Hope's plate. 'It's nice just having lunch the two of us, isn't it? We need to make the most of it, before you go to big-girl school.'

'Hope go to big-girl school?' Hope asked.

'Not yet, don't worry. We've got plenty more time for lunches together before that,' Holly said, although it was hard not to think about how quickly the time had gone. No doubt it would feel like only a blink of an eye had passed when Hope was dressed in her uniform and Holly was waving her off for her first day of school. Yes, they would need to do plenty of these lunches before then.

Maybe some nice long weekends too, although she didn't really know where. Evan was far better at picking things like that.

The thought of Evan caused Holly's stomach to jolt. She was meant to be enjoying her time with Hope, not feeling sorry for herself, but no sooner had she opened her mouth to speak again, than her phone buzzed on the table.

Holly had received several messages from Fin that morning, saying that it would be fine for her to come around at whatever time she wanted. She'd also had a couple from Jamie too, saying that she was happy to look after Hope for a few hours if Holly and Fin wanted a bit of time alone with Anne. But so far, Holly hadn't replied with anything more than smiley-faced emojis. The only reason she and Fin would need time alone with Anne would be to sort out the funeral, and that was something Holly didn't want to face. And so she continued to help Hope colour in her placemat, ignoring the world beyond the café walls.

Hope had just finished eating when another message came through. One far harder to brush aside.

> Can't wait to meet you and my granddaughter.
> Anne x

Holly put her cutlery down on the plate. She couldn't avoid it any longer. She needed to see Anne.

While Hope was perfectly capable of walking, Holly decided to carry her back to the car. Being carried was something that happened solely on Hope's agenda and normally she resisted, but the large meal had made her sleepy and Holly knew that someday, she'd be too big to carry. The last thing she wanted was to miss out on those moments.

It was when Holly was buckling her daughter into the car seat that Hope asked the one question Holly dreaded more than any other.

'Is Evvy home?' Hope asked. 'Hope wants Evvy.'

Holly inched away from the car, as she racked her mind for what to say. They were about to see Anne. Evan's own mother. Maybe this was as good a moment as Holly was going to get to break the news.

She opened her mouth, feeling her pulse drumming in her ears. Her hands were trembling. It would pass, Holly told herself. All this pain would pass. She just had to do this. She just had to get the words out. Drawing a deep breath in, Holly looked her daughter in the eye.

'No, darling, Evvy's not home at the minute,' she said.

Hope nodded with a seriousness that was far beyond someone of her young age.

'He's on a plane,' she said matter-of-factly. Of course that was what Hope would think. Whenever Evan was away travelling, they always said he was on a plane. It was far easier than expecting Hope to understand the names of all the different countries he went to. A lump swelled in Holly's chest. The pulsing in her ears stuttering as she drew in another breath. She couldn't. She couldn't do it.

'Yes, Hopey, he's on a plane,' she said. 'Evvy's on a plane.'

'He'll be back soon?'

Holly blinked away the tears, wiping her eyes as she tried to force it all down.

'That's right, Hope. Evvy is on a plane and he'll be home soon.'

19

When Evan had first introduced Holly to his mother on a video call only days after first meeting him, Holly had been struck by how glamorous Anne was. She knew from Evan being the joint youngest in his family – he was the only boy in a set of triplets – that Anne was likely older than Holly's own mother. And yet she had looked a decade younger, with her hair perfectly blow-dried and subtle makeup that hid any trace of wrinkles. That was the person Holly had spoken to time and again since then on video calls, and it was the person she expected to see when she stepped into Fin's living room several hours after leaving her home. While the woman she greeted looked similar in both hair colour and build, she was far, far frailer than the one Holly had seen on the screen, with red-rimmed eyes, sunken-in cheeks and narrow lips that trembled the instant she saw Holly.

'Oh, Holly. I'm—'

'I'm so sorry, Anne,' Holly said, determined not to have that preface to her name used again, and instead, turning it back around on Evan's mother. 'I'm so sorry.'

'Oh, hon, I can't—'

Whatever Anne was going to say was cut short as she stopped mid-sentence and covered her hand with her mouth, though she was no longer looking at Holly. She was looking at Hope, who was standing in the doorway. With tears gleaming in her eyes, and an encroaching smile lighting up her face, Anne crouched down.

'Hope, Hope. Oh, darling Hope!' she exclaimed as she stretched out her arms for a hug. 'You sweetheart. It's your granny. You know me, don't you? It's Granny Annie.'

Knowing exactly what Anne needed, Hope stepped forward and let herself be engulfed by her grandmother's embrace. Although when she finally realised who it was she was hugging, Hope shuffled back and looked up at Anne with large, wide eyes.

'Granny bring present?' Hope grinned.

'Hope!' Holly said, not sure if she should laugh or cry. She was still struggling with having Anne there, in front of her. She'd seen so much of her on the screen over the previous eighteen months, but each of those times, Evan had been there with her. And now, the first time they were meeting face to face, he wasn't there. He'd never be there again. Still, the horrendous circumstances weren't going to deter Hope from getting what she wanted.

'Evvy said Granny bring presents,' Hope tried again.

'Is that right?' Anne chuckled as she stood up. Her smile was so broad, it made Holly's cheeks ache, and yet the tears were streaming down the older woman's face. 'Well, I might have brought one or two things, but I came very quickly, so I didn't remember them all. I'll bring more next time, okay? Next time.'

'When Evvy's back from his plane?' Hope said matter-of-factly.

Anne's eyes flickered from Hope to Holly, who tried not to show the tension that had locked on her shoulders.

Quickly avoiding the gaze, Holly smiled down at her daughter.

'Hopey, why don't you go find Uncle Fin? You go find Uncle Fin and Aunty Jamie. They're in the kitchen, okay? Granny and I are going to sit down. We need to have a chat. Is that all right?'

Hope gave a relaxed shrug. She was perfectly comfortable moving around Jamie and Fin's home, almost as if she knew this was where she'd lived when she was first born.

'Hey, Hopey, how do you fancy practising some skateboarding in here?' Holly heard Fin say.

Knowing that her daughter was in safe hands, Holly moved across to the armchair and took a seat. This was it. This was where she had to describe, yet again, how she had watched Evan die.

Silence swelled around them. Holly and Anne were sitting in opposite corners of the living room with Holly on the armchair that was tucked in next to the fire while Anne looked tiny on the mammoth cushions of the sofa. When Holly had first moved into this house and it had only been her and Jamie, they would often sit like this, with one of them lounging on the sofa, and the other sitting on the armchair, with their feet up on the footstool. And it had always felt perfectly relaxed. But it didn't now. Now the room felt unbearably warm, unbearably large, and even with the radiators blasting out heat, Holly couldn't shift the chill that surrounded her.

'Anne—'

'Oh my goodness, he did it. He did it, didn't he?'

For a split second, Holly thought she was talking about Evan saving the boy, but as she looked up, she noticed how Evan's mum was staring at her hand, or more precisely at the ring on her left finger, the same way her mother had done the day before.

Holly glanced down at her hand. It felt like such a normal thing to do when she first put the ring on. It had felt natural, even when she told her mother. But now, here in front of Evan's mum, she felt like some immature schoolgirl, who was playing pretend marriage with a man she would never wed. She felt like a fraud.

'Actually, he didn't get round to it. He brought it with him. It was in his pocket when he went in the water.'

20

Holly didn't know how Anne was going to react. For a second, Holly feared she might erupt and tell her to take the ring off or snatch it off her hand herself. Perhaps she would scream that Holly wasn't deserving of Evan's love and it was her fault he was dead. It wouldn't have been the type of thing the Anne Holly knew would say, but really, how well did she know this woman?

Evan's mother stood up and walked over to the armchair before she crouched down, wrapped her arms around Holly and sobbed.

Anne was the only one crying and Holly just felt so out of place. It was that same feeling she had experienced earlier outside the sweet shop, as if her mind and body had separated from each other. But Anne needed this, and Anne was Evan's mother. That was all that mattered.

When the older woman finally broke away, she wiped her eyes and sniffed, looking at Holly apologetically.

'I'm sorry, honey. I shouldn't have unburdened myself like that on you,' she said.

Holly's heart throbbed with a pain that, for once, wasn't her own. 'I understand.'

'Of course you do. And I'm glad you're wearing the ring. He bought it for you. That was what you were meant to do. And thank you for the lovely hamper of sweets you sent over too. That was very generous of you.'

Holly smiled gratefully, still unsure what she would have done if Anne had asked her to take the ring off.

'I don't know what I'm supposed to do,' Holly said honestly. 'I don't know how I'm supposed to go about my day. We had all these plans, you know, and now I just have to... what? Hang about and wait for the funeral? I don't even know what I'm doing there. I've never planned a funeral. I don't want to plan a funeral.'

'I can help. That's what I'm here for.' Anne smiled softly, but Holly couldn't reciprocate. No parent wanted to bury their own child and there was no need for the event to be more stressful for Anne than it had to be. Not with so many of them there in Bourton, on hand to help.

As if hearing her thoughts, there was a light tap on the door. Both women turned to find Fin standing there.

'Hey, I just brought you some teas,' he said. Fin might not be British, but he'd adopted the fact that there were some situations that required a sweet, milky tea.

As he placed the drinks down on the coffee table, he carried on speaking.

'I heard what you two were saying about the funeral,' he said. 'I didn't mean to listen in. It's just harder to knock on a door with two mugs of tea in your hand than you'd think.'

Holly let out a short chuckle that felt conspicuously awkward. Thankfully, Fin just carried on.

'I just wanted to say that I've already started the process and I'm happy to keep going with it.'

'Sorry?' Holly said, not sure she understood.

'I emailed some local funeral homes this morning when I couldn't sleep. I just felt like I should do something and contacting them seemed like the most useful thing.'

'Fin, thank you, you didn't have to do that. I'm sure you didn't want to,' Holly said.

To her surprise, Fin answered quite forcefully. 'Actually, I did. I do. Really. It's the last thing I can do for him, you know, make sure it goes okay. But I get it if you want to take over. That's fine. We can work together.'

Holly shook her head, surprised to find a fraction of the weight that had been pressing down on her chest had lifted slightly. The funeral hadn't really entered her thoughts, but that was because she had avoided thinking about it. Having Fin take over was something she hadn't known she'd needed until that moment.

'No, it's fine. I'm happy to leave it to you, if you're sure you don't mind? You knew him for longer. You would know what he'd like.'

'Thank you, Fin,' Anne said, reaching out and taking his hand.

He smiled weakly and kissed Anne on the cheek.

'I should let you guys talk,' he said. 'But we're here if you need anything. Anything at all.'

A moment later, he was walking out of the room and once again leaving Holly on her own with Anne.

21

Holly was worried that silence was going to settle again, but Anne straightened her back and offered Holly a strained smile. It certainly wasn't as genuine as the one she had given Hope when she first hugged her, but Holly could hardly blame her for that. In Holly's opinion, it was a miracle Anne was managing to smile at all.

'I brought a photo album,' Anne said. 'I don't know why. It's only a small one, and it's got pictures of the girls in too. It's probably only got a couple of photos of Evan. All the big ones are in the loft. It was before the days of phones and photos on computers, of course. It seems silly now. Bringing it all the way here when I don't even know what's in it. It's just when I was packing, I was thinking of Hope, thinking how much she was going to miss him, and I don't know. It seemed like a good idea, but no, it's ridiculous. You probably think I'm ridiculous.'

'No, I don't,' Holly said genuinely. 'I think it's incredibly thoughtful of you to think of Hope like that. And I'd very much like to see it, if that's okay?'

This time, the smile that creased Anne's face reached her eyes, though they quickly glazed with tears. 'Yes, of course. It's just upstairs. I'll only be a minute. Although I think I need to pop to the bathroom and put a face back on while I'm up there. You don't mind, do you?'

'Of course not,' Holly said, wishing there was something more she could say to take Anne's hurt away. 'I'll see if I can hunt down some biscuits to go with these teas while you're upstairs.'

'That sounds wonderful.'

While Anne disappeared to find the album and fix her makeup, Holly went into the kitchen, where Fin was currently still helping Hope on the skateboard. Jamie was resting her chin on her hands as she watched them and for a second, Holly just observed the scene. It was all so relaxed. So normal. No outsider would be able to tell the agony that was hidden beneath the surface of all the joyful smiles. For a moment longer, Holly continued to watch, when Jamie suddenly turned around. Startled, she jumped at the sight of Holly, grabbing her bump as she did.

'Is everything okay?' she asked, quickly straightening herself up. 'Where's Anne?'

'She popped upstairs to find a photo album she brought. I think she wanted to put a bit of makeup on, too.'

Jamie nodded, though she didn't say anything. There was no way Holly could deal with another silence, even if it was with her best friend, and so she carried on talking.

'I said I'd see if you had any biscuits. It doesn't matter if you don't. I should have brought some of the things I baked yesterday with Hope. If I'd had my head on straight, I would have remembered the blondies.'

'I don't think anyone is expecting you to have your head on straight at the moment,' Jamie said, making no attempt to hide the worry on her face.

Holly wasn't going to reply, but out the corner of her eye, she watched as Hope pushed one foot along the ground and set the skateboard moving the way Fin had shown her to. As Hope rolled into Fin's arms, she jumped onto the floor and clapped in delight.

'*She* is,' Holly said, finally responding to Jamie's comment. 'She's expecting life to carry on as normal, and she needs it to. And there's the shop to think of. That still needs running.'

'You have Caroline there. And your dad. You need to think about yourself. Take time for yourself. You won't be good for anyone if you don't.'

Holly mulled the point over as she continued to watch Hope. It was all well and good for Jamie to say that Holly needed to put herself first and that others could pick up the slack, but Caroline had a family of her own to look after, and she wasn't paid to be a manager. As for her father, the best thing Holly could do for Arthur was show him she was okay. That was what she needed to do. She couldn't afford to crumble and fall apart. Not when she had responsibilities.

From upstairs came the sound of running water, and Holly found herself needing to get out of the kitchen away from the pressure of Jamie's concern.

'Sorry,' she said, making sure there was a smile on her face as she spoke. 'Did you say you have some biscuits or not?'

22

When Anne returned to the living room, she looked like an entirely different person. There was colour on her cheeks, courtesy of masterfully applied strokes of blush, gloss on her lips and a dark-brown mascara that made her eyes look double the size. It would have been enough to fool most people. Only there was still that tight, strained twist to her lips, and the way her eyes didn't crease when she smiled, which stopped her from looking entirely at ease.

'I had a quick flick through, and there are a couple of good ones of him in here,' Anne said, taking a place on the sofa next to Holly. 'I hadn't realised it was an album full of the triplets. Thick as thieves they were.'

She opened up the first page, and Holly let out an involuntary laugh.

'Oh my goodness, they must have been such hard work!'

The photo she was looking at was of three children, around six months of age, sitting on the floor with what appeared to be flour all over them. Evan was easily identifiable as the one in blue, while his two sisters wore the same style babygrow in pink.

'He was so cute,' Holly said, unable to draw her gaze away from those glistening eyes and cheerful cheeks. 'He looks like such a happy baby.'

'Oh, honey, he was a happy baby, all right,' Anne said. 'But he was a terror, mind. Could be an absolute nightmare when he wanted to be. He'd got his sisters wrapped around his little finger from the day he was born, and me too. Oh yes. He'd got me wrapped around his finger, the lot of us. And Jonathan... Well, Evan was the apple of his father's eye. Gosh, our Evan was a charmer from the day he was born.'

Holly turned over a page in the album to a picture where a far older Evan was now standing up on the top of a tyre swing while his triplet sisters squeezed into the centre together.

'I guess he was about six or seven in this one,' Anne told Holly. 'He broke his arm on that tyre swing, you know? We'd had it in the garden for years. All the girls used to play on it. Even our eldest Catherine played on it for years. None of them broke so much as a pinkie. But Evan didn't do things by halves. No, he catapulted himself from the top one afternoon. Standing on it like he's doing there. He didn't tell us how bad it hurt though. No, he didn't want to get into trouble, so he just hid it. It wasn't until I spotted how he couldn't put his coat on that I took him to the emergency room.' Anne laughed sadly as she shook her head and Holly couldn't help but think that it sounded like the type of mischievous thing Hope would do – pretend she was absolutely fine to avoid getting into trouble.

'It's still in the garden, you know,' Anne carried on. 'That very same tyre and rope. I kept thinking about replacing it, but then the first grandkids came along. You know, Catherine's and Melissa's, and they all love it. They won't let me change it now. Not even the grotty old rope. God, they all love that swing. I even thought that maybe one day you and Evan would bring Hope and, and...'

Anne's words came to a stuttering stop and any trace of light in her eyes faded.

And... Holly knew exactly what Anne hadn't been able to say. And Evan's children. That was what she'd hoped. She'd wished that one day, Holly and Evan would bring Hope and all their other children over to play on that same tyre swing where their father had broken his arm. But those other children would never exist now. And neither did Evan.

'I would love to see it,' Holly said, forcing herself to speak before the grief became too overwhelming. 'I would love to see all these places that he talked about. He has so many amazing memories of where he grew up. Had.' She corrected herself, though it was like sticking a dagger between her ribs. 'Had so many amazing memories of all these places.'

And that was when the thought clicked. It was like turning on a light switch.

Over the past three days, Holly's mind had been nothing but a blur, but all of a sudden, she could see everything crystal clear. She knew what she had to do.

'Let's do it,' she said, facing Anne and taking her hands.

Anne shook her head, confused. 'Do what?'

'Take me to America. Let's go back to America. Let's take Hope and go together. Now.'

23

Holly's heart was pounding and, for the first time since she had lost Evan, it wasn't out of fear. It was out of excitement. She could feel it. The adventure buzzing beneath her skin, although when she looked at Anne, she found her lips were pressed tightly together, as if she hadn't understood what Holly had said.

'I want you to show me these places,' Holly said, forcing herself to speak slowly. Though it wasn't easy. Her pulse was hammering away as adrenaline rushed through her veins. 'It'll be two weeks until the funeral. Isn't that how long these things normally take? Sometimes it's longer, lots longer. Let me come back to the States with you? See these places Evan loved. See this tyre swing.' She tapped on the picture in the photo album. 'It's got to be better than just waiting around, hasn't it?'

As she waited for Anne's answer, silence swirled around them. Anne's lips were still tightly pressed together, and now a deep furrow had formed between her brows.

'That's a lovely idea, Holly, but really, I don't think it's sensible. Surely you want to be here, with Hope?'

'I'll bring Hope with us. It makes perfect sense. I don't want to be here. I *can't* be here. I need to be with Evan somehow. I need to learn these things about him that I never got to learn while he was alive. This way I can do that. This is what I think I should do. No, scrap that. I *know* I should do this.'

Holly could feel it. She could feel in her bones that this was the right thing, and now she knew what she needed to do. She didn't want to waste another minute.

Jumping to her feet, she opened the living room door and called out towards the kitchen.

'Fin, can you come here for a minute, please?'

Fin sprinted into the living room, panic his only expression. 'What is it? Is everything okay?'

'It's nothing, it's nothing,' Holly said. 'Honestly, it's just... Did you mean what you said about taking care of everything? Taking care of the funeral and not needing me to do anything?'

'Of course I did. Why?'

'And you don't mind me leaving everything up to you?'

Fin tilted his head to the side quizzically.

'If that's what feels best for you, then of course I don't mind. Why? What is it you need?'

'Nothing. Nothing else anyway,' Holly assured him as a flutter of excitement built within her. 'It's just, I want to take Hope to America. I want us to see where Evan grew up. I want to meet all his family. And I want to do it as soon as possible, as long as you're okay with that?'

It was only while Holly was waiting for Fin's answer that she realised Anne hadn't actually said whether it was okay. Holly looked at Anne with a sudden flash of guilt, thinking about how much she'd railroaded the old woman. After all, it was ridiculous her trying to make arrangements if Anne hadn't even agreed to host her.

'As long as you don't mind?' she added.

Anne drew a deep breath in and Holly felt her pulse kick up a notch. She wasn't sure what she'd do if Anne said she didn't want them to come, but at the same time, she could fully understand why that would be the case. The poor woman had just lost her son and flown halfway across the world. The last thing she was going to want to do was fly all the way back, with her dead son's not-quite-fiancée and a toddler. Yet as Holly held her breath, a small smile flickered onto Anne's expression.

'I think it's a lovely idea,' she said at last. 'If I'm honest, I don't really know how I was hoping to help here. I thought it would be good, being with you all, especially being with Hope, but I've only just landed and all I can think about is how I should have stayed at home with Jonathan and the girls. And this way, Hope could meet her cousins. I mean, they're not cousins exactly, they're—'

'They're cousins,' Holly confirmed. The more she thought about it, the more certain she felt. 'And you're right – I think it would be perfect. I think that's exactly what we should do. So, you're all right to arrange the funeral?' she said, looking once again at Fin. His face was crumpled into a mass of frown lines as he looked between Holly and Anne and back again.

'I am,' he said, 'but I don't think it's going to be quite as simple to leave as you think.'

24

The troops had been gathered at remarkable speed, and every one of them was there, filling Jamie's living room. Anne was looking after the children, while Ben, Michael, Giles, Caroline and even Georgia joined Jamie and Fin to give Holly advice on her idea. Although it didn't really feel like advice, it felt like they were all telling her exactly what she was and wasn't allowed to do with her life.

'Absolutely not.' Those were the first words out of Jamie's mouth when Holly told her. A point she reinforced when they all got together. 'Holly, you are not thinking straight in any way. This is not a good idea.'

'I know you don't see this, but at some point, the grief is going to hit you for real,' Caroline said, her voice slightly more measured than Jamie's.

'You don't think I'm grieving?' Holly replied sharply.

'Not properly, no, I don't think you are,' Caroline said, with the same measured thoughtfulness. 'And I think when that grief really hits, you need to be at home, surrounded by people you love. Surrounded by your family.'

'All I'm doing is being pragmatic,' Holly protested. 'Me becoming a blubbering mess isn't going to change anything. It won't help Hope and it certainly won't help me. Evan's family is my family too. Or at least they would have been had he had a chance to, to...' She sniffed forcefully, swallowing back the emotion she felt along with the word she wasn't yet ready to say. She wasn't going to get teary through this; that wasn't what she wanted. She wanted to put across her most factual, organised, persuasive speech to make them see she was right.

'What about the shop?' Ben said. 'It's Christmas time. The busiest period of the year. You can't want to leave now.'

'I think it's the perfect time to leave, actually,' Holly said. 'You know how news spreads through the village. All the locals'll be coming in wanting to have conversations about Evan, filling up the shop and not letting me serve actual customers.'

Holly decided not to mention the fact she hadn't even been able to go into the shop that morning. This wasn't the time for that. This was a time to convince them all that she was going to be fine. She knew she was going to be far better off in America than staying here, and she was finding it hard to understand why they didn't see that.

'Drey's gonna come into the shop,' Holly said, addressing Ben's initial concern. 'She's already on her holiday. She'll work as much as I need her. I know she will. But regardless of that, I don't want to be in that shop. I don't want to be in this county or this country. I want to be away from it and I want to be with Evan's family.'

Silence fell between them as the group exchanged a flurry of looks. It was almost as if they thought Holly couldn't see the way they were looking at each other. The way they were communicating about her, when she was standing right beside them.

'I can take a week off work,' Ben said finally.

'Sorry?' Holly said.

'I've got a week of holiday that I can take. Georgia and I had planned on doing something, but it's fine. That's not a problem.' He glanced at Georgia, who nodded swiftly.

'Absolutely. You should go with her.'

'Ben, I don't want to take your holiday.'

'No, but you want to take my daughter across the other side of the world when you're in an emotionally stressed state? That's not gonna happen. If you want to go, I get it. I understand it. But my condition for taking Hope is that you take me too. Okay? It means it can only be a week, but it's the best I can agree to right now.'

Holly sank back in her chair. She didn't like how Ben had referred to her as being in *an emotionally stressed state*, considering how rational she was being about everything, but there was no way she could take Hope out of the country without his blessing and permission, and there was no way she could be parted from Hope at the moment.

'One week?' She said it as much to herself as to the group. She didn't know much about America, but she knew it was big and that travelling between places could take days, sometimes longer, which meant they would only really be able to go to one place: Evan's childhood home, outside Seattle.

Holly countered with a suggestion of her own. 'What about if you stay with me for the first week and then, if you see that I'm doing okay, you let me stay on for another week on my own?'

Ben shook his head. 'No. Caroline is right. When grief really hits, you're gonna need people. You're gonna need...' He back-tracked, seeing Holly's glare already forming. 'You're going to need people who really know you to be on hand. It doesn't matter that they're family, Holly. I get that. I get they are your family, but they still don't know you like we do and that matters in this case. I know you understand that.'

Holly did. She fully understood where they were coming from,

and the fact that Ben was being so reasonable was hardly something she could ignore.

'I guess that'll have to be enough,' she said quietly. 'One week
to see where Evan grew up.'

25

Holly was excited. She was going to America. It was a place that had always been on her bucket list, though she doubted she'd ever get there until she'd met Evan. Before she'd known him, Holly would have considered a trip to France exotic, but with Evan by her side, the world really had become her oyster. America was somewhere she was certain they would have gone at some point, given the amount of family Evan had there. Of course, this wasn't the way she'd imagined doing it, with her not-quite-mother-in-law, along with her ex-boyfriend and daughter, less than a week after her not-quite-fiancé had died. But that didn't change the fact that it was going to be an adventure.

'It's not too late to back out,' Ben said, as they stood in the line, ready to check their luggage in. It had taken two days to get everything sorted. Two days that had felt even more of a blur than the previous ones, but at least these were a blur with focus – what with finding flights to packing enough warm clothes for Hope, there was barely a minute to sit and think about Evan. Now they were at the airport and Holly couldn't help but feel a bubble of excitement within her. A bubble Ben seemed determined to burst.

'No one's going to think any less of you if you decide you want to stay,' he said. 'People often make strange decisions when they're grieving. That's okay.'

Holly felt her jaw lock, but rather than responding, she turned and looked at Anne.

'I'm still okay to go, as long as you're still all right with having us, Anne?'

'Of course, of course. I think you're right – it's good. I think us doing this together will be good. It's a distraction, a way to stop us thinking, I guess.'

'Is Evvy on the plane?' Hope said as she tugged on Holly's hand. 'Mamma, is this Evvy's plane?'

Holly bit down on her lip. As soon as Hope found out she was going on a plane, her first comment had been about seeing Evan, and Holly had fielded dozens of comments like this already. Each time, Holly had noticed the way Ben and Anne's eyes avoided both hers and Hope's. Liked they disapproved of Holly's way of handling the situation. But how could she tell Hope what had really happened? She wouldn't understand. It wouldn't be fair. It was better for Hope to think that he was travelling, constantly travelling, until maybe one day she didn't miss him quite as much. That was the hope, at least.

'Not on this plane, Hopey,' Holly said, taking her daughter's hand. 'But I think there are going to be a lot of fun things for us to see and do. I think you're going to be able to see clouds and houses and birds.'

'Birds in the sky and planes in the sky?'

'You're right, they are in the sky.'

'And Evvy? I want to see Evvy. Is he in the sky? Hope misses Evvy.'

'I know... Soon, okay, Hopey? I'm sure you'll see him soon.'

Holly felt the lump build in her throat but as she went to swallow it, a sharp hiss caught her attention.

'Anne,' Ben, who was the source of the hissing sound, said. 'Are you all right looking after Hope for a second?'

'Of course. Absolutely.'

'Why? I can stay with her. I'm not going anywhere?' Holly said, but she had barely finished when Ben took hold off her by the elbow and pulled her out of the queue.

With Ben still holding on to her, they weaved in between people and luggage and it was only when they were standing over by a stack of trolleys that Ben let go and twisted around to face her. It wasn't very often that Holly saw Ben get angry. In fact, other than the very first time they had met, when she had accidentally run out onto the road and in front of his bike, she could rarely recall a single time. But she knew at that moment, he was angry.

'You've got to tell her. You have to tell Hope about Evan. It's not fair.'

Holly's molars ground together. In an instant, her anger had matched Ben's and multiplied.

'You want to talk to me about what's fair?' she said. 'I just lost the love of my life.'

'I understand, but Hope lost someone she loved too, and she doesn't even know it. All these places you're going to, all these stories you're going to hear about Evan, and you're just going to tell her what? He's still on a plane? How long is he going to stay on a plane for?'

Holly shook her head.

'I don't know, but it's not the right time to tell her now. It's not.'

'It's being cruel, Holly, and it's being selfish. I hate saying this to you right now. I do. I know how much you're going through, honestly, but surely you've got to see this is selfish. You're delaying her hurt. Delaying her opportunity to miss him and grieve. Evan was the love of your life; I get that. But Hope is my daughter too, and if you're not going to tell her, then I am.'

26

It was a horrific altercation to have at any time, but particularly before they had to sit on a plane for thirteen hours next to one another.

'Are you all right if I sit in the aisle?' Anne asked as they boarded the plane. 'I just need a little more room to stretch my legs.'

'Yes, of course, that's fine,' Holly said.

They had booked the four centre seats, and without checking Ben minded, Holly took the aisle on the other side. Thankfully, there was Hope to sit in between the pair of them. Since Ben had commented that Holly needed to tell their daughter about Evan, Holly hadn't said a single word to him. She couldn't. She could hardly even bear to look at him. The fact that he had threatened to tell Hope himself made her even more furious. Thankfully, keeping Hope busy while they went through to the departure gate and then waited to board had meant there had been more than enough to occupy her while she avoided speaking to Ben. But now it wasn't going to be so easy.

'Please, Holly, you have to understand,' Ben started, before the plane had even taken off.

'Don't. Don't do it. Not right now. I don't want to talk to you about it.'

He nodded solemnly. 'I just want what's best.'

'Please.' Holly clamped her hands over Hope's ears and glared at him. 'I know. I heard you. But really, this is not the place to have this conversation. Do you want me to do it here? Now?'

'Maybe it'll be easier that way,' Ben said. 'She knows Evan used to go on lots of planes. Maybe she'll feel close to him.'

Holly shook her head and grunted, unable to believe that he could say something so hard and callous. Only was it? Ben wasn't the callous type. And he'd never suggest anything if he thought it would hurt Hope. So why was he suggesting this?

Holly sat back in her seat, waiting for take-off. She had her fingers crossed that Hope would sleep for a chunk of the flight, but had packed plenty of colouring books and games to keep her occupied if she stayed awake. And if all else failed, the iPad was fully loaded with her favourite shows.

As it happened, the flight went better than Holly could have dreamed. Hope fussed a little during take-off, her ears struggling to adjust to the change in pressure, but it didn't take long before she was perfectly relaxed. The attendants were lovely, everyone flashing a quick smile at Hope and usually offering her a sweet treat every time they passed. Hope smiled obligingly each time, and with perfect manners said thank you, giving no indication that her mother owned a sweet shop and that Holly had packed enough sugar to feed the entire plane, although much of that was for gifts.

When Hope fell asleep, Holly was sure Ben was going to bring up the topic again, and so she put on her headphones and switched on a film, turning the volume up high so she wouldn't hear if he did try to talk to her. At some point, during her second or third film, she did actually fall asleep, and it was only when the wheels of the plane bumped on the tarmac that she woke up.

'Oh my goodness! Hope!' Holly said, glancing to her side, only to find that her daughter wasn't there. Her heart lurched for a split second, before she saw her, one seat along, chatting away with her grandmother. Ben must have swapped places so she could be by Anne. Holly's stomach churned. She didn't want to have the conversation. Not now. Not ever, really. And as the plane taxied across the runway, Ben remained quiet on the matter, asking Holly only if she slept well, and telling her what Hope had eaten while she was sleeping. For a couple of minutes, Holly thought Ben might actually have used the time flying to consider what he had asked of her, and come to the conclusion that Holly was in the right. However, when they stood by the conveyer belt waiting for their luggage, she discovered that wasn't the case at all.

27

Hope was with Anne, looking at the flight and conveyer belt numbers on the large screen. Given that they had only just walked off the plane, Holly knew there was going to be a bit of a wait until their bags arrived. Apparently, Ben took that to mean it was the perfect time to force his agenda again.

'Holly, I don't mean to push you,' he started, which Holly took as a sure sign to mean he did, 'but in a minute, Evan's father is going to greet you and there's a good chance he's going to be upset. Then when we get to the house, you guys are going to meet all of Evan's sisters. Not to mention his nieces and nephews, who will all already know what happened. They're going to be upset too, and Hope's going to want to know why. You know how sensitive she is to things like this. It makes no sense to hide it from her. Not when she's going to be surrounded by people who will all be talking about the fact that Evan has gone and wanting to comfort her.'

As much as she didn't want to, Holly could see Ben's side of things. To a small extent, at least. Hope was perceptive when it came to people's emotions. She knew when Holly had been worrying about her father, Arthur, or when Evan had had a lot on his plate work wise. And that was without anyone even saying anything directly to her. Perhaps she could just tell Evan's family to not mention Evan's death around Hope, but she dismissed the idea almost immediately. How was that something she could even monitor unless she was with Hope the entire time? And what would she do if one of Evan's sisters, like Ben, decided Hope had a right to know? Where would that leave her?

'Do you just want me to do it now?' Holly said, her voice exasperated and exhausted. 'Do you want me to tell her here while everyone's collecting their bags?'

Ben shrugged. 'There's never going to be a right time, Holly. There won't be. There will never be a right time or a right place. And if you want me to do it for you—'

'No!' Holly snapped as she shook her head. 'Of course I don't.'

She could feel anger burning in her, but it was anger trying to mask something else. Something much, much more painful.

'I just don't know how,' she said finally, letting the words out with a long sigh. 'I just don't know how to do it.'

Ben nodded and touched her elbow. It wasn't the same way as he had grabbed her before. He wasn't trying to make Holly listen to him. He was trying to show her he was listening instead.

'I'll be there, Holly,' he said quietly. 'I'll be right there beside you the entire time. But you need to do this. You need to do this now.'

28

This couldn't be her life, Holly thought, as they walked over to a bench, near where dozens of trolleys were neatly clipped together and several conveyor belts were moving sluggishly with various arrays of luggage on them. Holly's life was meant to be a simple one – Hope and Evan, the sweet shop, their friends, the Cotswolds. That was what she'd envisioned. Not this. Not sitting in a foreign airport luggage lounge, about to tell her daughter that the man she thought of as a father was never coming back.

Ben sat on the other side of Hope, but Holly knew he wouldn't say anything, not unless she needed him to, and right now, it wasn't a case of what Holly needed anyway, it was a case of what Hope needed, and what Hope needed was for her mother to be strong.

'Hope, lots of people have been a little bit sad recently. Have you noticed that?'

Hope nodded, her little chin wobbling up and down. 'Aunty JayJay cried,' she said. 'And Uncle Fin. And Nanny Annie. They sad.'

'Yes, they were sad,' Holly said, clenching her fist to stop it from trembling.

'They lose something?' Hope said, jumping to the most logical conclusion for her. Hope was always losing teddies and toys and each time, she would be in floods of tears until Holly found the missing item, which was almost inevitably shoved down the back of the sofa, or under her bed.

'Oh God,' Holly said, before deciding to take Hope's lead. 'I suppose. I suppose they did. Yes, they did lose something.'

'A toy? Aunty JayJay lose toy?'

'Well—'

'Mamma find it. Mamma find JayJay's toy.'

Holly held her breath, wishing she could stop time. Stop time just long enough to gather herself and work out how she was going to do this. This method of saying Evan was lost wouldn't work. Hope believed with unwavering faith that Holly could find any item misplaced. That wouldn't be any different when she told Hope it was Evan they'd lost.

With a sharp inhalation, Holly sniffed back her tears. She knew at some point, she would break, that the tears would run freely and unstoppably, but she needed to hold off for as long as she could. She needed Hope to see her being strong.

'No, darling, the thing is, people are sad because something's happened. Sometimes, when people get sick, or old...' Holly swallowed her words back, immediately regretting them. Evan wasn't sick or old; he was young and healthy, and this shouldn't have happened. She tried again. 'Sometimes, for no reason that seems fair to any of us, people have to go.'

'Go? Go to work?'

Holly pressed her lips together and glanced up at Ben, who nodded encouragingly.

'A little bit like that, maybe. Not exactly,' Holly stuttered.

'When people go like this, they can't come back. They don't have a choice. It's not because they wanted to go. Evan didn't want to go, Hopey, but he didn't have a choice. He was very brave, and he saved someone. He saved someone, but that means we had to lose him. Do you understand? He saved someone.'

Hope didn't understand. Holly could see that from the concerned looks she was giving both her mother and father. Somehow, Holly needed to explain things better, but she didn't know how. She was doing the best she could, but it wasn't good enough. It wasn't enough.

With a deep breath in, she clasped her daughter's hands tightly and closed her eyes. She needed to say it. She needed to say the words, but once she did, there would be no coming back.

Fighting the skipping beats of her heart, she opened her eyes and looked up to a screen that was announcing the conveyor belt numbers for different flights. She just needed a minute. A minute to gather her thoughts. She had seen Evan in his final moments. She had been there alone in a hospital when she lost him. Not to mention the fact that she'd told his best friend about his death and looked his mother in the eye wearing an engagement ring Evan had never got to give her. Holly would not break at this. She wouldn't.

Drawing on all the strength she had, Holly looked back at Hope.

'We just have to be strong, Hopey,' she said, forcing herself to smile. 'And we will be. Evvy's gone. And he can't come back.'

'Evvy's on a plane?' Hope said, but Holly shook her head. 'Evvy home soon?'

'No, darling. Evvy can't come home again. I'm sorry. I'm very, very sorry.'

29

Just like with Anne, Holly had seen Jonathan on the screen plenty of times before and the moment they stepped through the electric doors into the arrivals, she spotted him. Jonathan was where Evan had got his height from, as he stood at well over six feet, but there was a frailness to him that Holly hadn't expected. A hunch to his shoulders and a paleness to his skin, although she suspected that happened to most people when they lost their son. As Ben hung back with the trolley and luggage, Anne was the first to greet her husband. The embrace was long and tender, but from what Holly could tell, the pair didn't exchange any words before they separated, at which point, Holly stepped towards him, holding Hope's hand.

'Jonathan,' Holly said, opening out an arm to offer him a hug, but before she could get there, Hope slipped out of her grip and jumped forward.

'Grandad!' she yelled excitedly, as if he was the person she had been waiting her whole life to see.

The old man's eyes began to water.

'Oh, Hope. I'm very pleased to meet you,' he said, crouching down to her level.

Hope had always been good with people, at least as a baby. It probably came from Holly having such a close-knit group of friends who would always look after her if she needed help. But the older Hope got, the more reticent she had become when it came to offering hugs. Holly was fine with that. It was better to have her child a little bit wary, she always thought, than happy to go off with anyone. However, there was no reticence or wariness at that moment. Instead, Hope flung herself into Jonathan's arms and a warmth Holly couldn't have expected flooded through her.

With the other three adults watching on, Jonathan stood back up, still holding Hope tightly as she fixed her arms securely around his neck.

'Well, isn't this something special?' Anne said, her face beaming as she pulled her phone out of her handbag. 'I think this is a memory we want to hold on to.'

'Grandad, Evvy's gone,' Hope said. 'Gone gone.' Tears filled Hope's eyes. Even though Holly knew her daughter hadn't fully understood the extent of what she'd been told, the thought of not seeing Evan again had been enough to make her bottom lip tremble. Thankfully, Holly had scooped her up in time to stop the tears falling, but now Jonathan was the one holding her and Holly couldn't just snatch her back.

Holly watched as the colour drained from Jonathan's face and the warmth she had felt only seconds ago evaporated, only to be replaced by the coldest chill of guilt and embarrassment.

'I'm sorry,' Holly said. 'Jonathan, I'm so sorry. We just told her... I only just—'

'It's fine,' Jonathan replied. 'It's not a problem.' He wasn't looking at Holly as he said this, though. Instead, he was still staring at Hope. 'You're right, Hope, my sweet, Evvy is gone. But you're here now, so you and Grandad are going to have a great time together, aren't we? You know, I think there might be a little present waiting back at the house for you. How does that sound?'

Without another word, Jonathan turned around, Hope still in his arms, and started walking. Anne was quickly on his heels. For a moment, Holly just watched them. The guilt and the warmth had both gone now, and in their place was a strange type of emptiness.

As Hope's laugh rattled through the air, Holly wished more than anything that Evan could see this. She wished he could have seen that first amazing interaction between Hope and her grandfather, how it had felt as if they'd known each other for years.

'Holly, are you okay?' Ben asked.

Holly blinked a couple of times, as if she had only just woken up, before looking at Ben, then looking back to Hope and her grandparents, who were now several feet ahead of them.

'Of course. Of course I'm fine. Come on. We don't want to keep them waiting.'

30

Holly didn't know what she'd imagined when she'd envisioned driving towards Evan's family home. She knew he lived outside the city, so she wasn't anticipating skyscrapers or anything like that, but she had some preconceived ideas in her mind. Most likely, she thought, he would live in one of those enormous homes she saw on so many American dramas, with three storeys, wooden façades, massive driveways, and manicured lawns that meant it was half a mile between the house and the roadside. Something pristine and elegant with wide pavements and nature stripped back in favour of select flowers and shrubbery chosen only for their aesthetic appeal. As it was, Holly quickly learned she had got it wrong. They were driving down a treelined road, where the houses were barely visible through the bare branches and trunks of deciduous trees, which seemed to get more and more densely packed the longer they drove. Holly couldn't tell if the houses hidden behind them had manicured lawns, but so far she'd not seen a single perfectly pruned hedge or pot plant.

'The lake is only a fifteen-minute walk away,' Anne said, flashing a smile back at Holly. 'It's a shame it's too cold to swim in at this time of year, but we can still go for a walk there. Next time you come, we'll go out on a boat, do some fishing, and have a barbecue afterwards. That was always one of Evan's favourite things to do. Mind you, he'd still be down there in three feet of snow if we'd let him. He never really felt the cold like the rest of us.'

Perhaps that was why he thought he'd be all right jumping into an icy lake, Holly reflected. Because he didn't think he'd feel the cold. But he'd felt the cold. He'd felt the ice and the freezing water so much, it had caused his organs to shut down.

'It sounds like a lovely place, Anne.'

It was Ben who spoke. His voice jolted through Holly and jerked her back into the moment. It took a second to remember what they had been talking about. Anne had spoken directly to her. She remembered that much. Yet, rather than replying, Holly's thoughts had drifted off. Drifted to Evan and the lake. That was it. Anne had been talking about the lake. About going out on a boat or something like that. Something Hope would definitely like to do.

'Yes, yes,' Holly said, with what was probably far too much enthusiasm. 'That does sound lovely.'

'Maybe in the summer, though,' Jonathan added. 'I don't think any of us will mind giving the lake a miss at the moment.'

Silence descended on the car, and a twist of guilt knotted in Holly's belly. It wasn't like she hadn't been thinking the same, or near enough. About Evan and the lake and losing him. But now Jonathan had voiced that thought, nobody knew how to respond. Tension was wrapping itself around the passengers in the car. Was this how the entire week was going to go? Brief conversations followed by awkward silences? Probably, but it would likely have been like that wherever she was. Sure, lakes were a particularly difficult subject, but really, it felt as though every part of her life was connected to Evan. At least this way, coming to America, Holly was being proactive. She was learning about Evan's life – which included the lakes he loved – meeting all his sisters and family, not to mention giving Hope a chance to meet them too.

No, she thought, straightening her back. This week was going to be positive. It was going to be positive and fun, for her and Hope and maybe even for Ben too.

She was about to ask Anne about all the things they could do locally, when Jonathan spoke again.

'Okay, well, this is us,' he said. They had taken a turning off the previous road and onto a narrow street that was more like a track than an actual road. The car rumbled over the stones, and after several minutes, when Holly was wondering where exactly they were heading, she saw it nestled in the trees. Their home. Evan's home.

31

In some ways, Holly had got it right. There was a manicured lawn, pristine hedgerows and sweeping driveway, but it wasn't in the way she had imagined. The building was two storeys, with the second floor's dormer windows breaking out of a dark tiled roof, which was in a stark contrast to the white of the rest of the house. Visually, the house was split into three different sections, which curved around in a horseshoe shape, but as mesmerising as the house was, it was the backdrop that held Holly's attention. Hundreds of trees, from every shade of green, through to oranges and browns, stretched out behind the building into dense woodland. At that moment, a slight mist had settled into the canopy, giving the entire place the feel of a fairy tale. Whatever Holly had envisioned, this surpassed those expectations a thousand times over.

'Is this where Evan grew up?' Holly asked, a sudden lightness filling her heart.

'Yes, he lived here all his life,' Anne replied. 'Well, before he went off to college and then to England, of course. I had all my kids here except Catherine.'

'Some weekends, it feels like we still have most of them living here, emptying the fridge,' Jonathan said gruffly, though Holly could hear the warmth in his tone. He didn't want it any other way. Especially not now.

'It's strange, you know,' Anne said as she carried on. 'I thought once they'd all left home, we'd downsize, get somewhere smaller, maybe with a view of the water. But Jonathan's right, they're always coming back, you know, and bringing the grandkids. I think Erin spends more time here than the flat she rents. And we look after Melissa's kids for a couple of days a week, too. It's nice for them to have their own space, you know, so we're not all on top of each other.'

Holly knew what she meant. When Evan had first come and stayed with her in Bourton, she had been living in the tiny cottage that Giles had bought for her unknowingly. It had been so wonderful having Evan there with her, waking up beside him, curling up in the evening on the sofa together. It was almost perfect. But the lack of space had been paramount in their decision to get something larger together.

'How are you feeling with the jet lag?' Anne asked. 'I guess that's one thing about my whistle-stop visit. I don't think I had a chance to get onto your time zone before I was flying back.'

As Holly considered the question, she found herself yawning. The idea of her being tired felt ridiculous, given all the hours she'd slept on the plane. But she'd never done a long-haul flight before. In fact, the furthest she'd ever gone abroad was to Evan's house in France, which they'd visited several times, including with Hope, but that was only an hour's time difference and they had just carried on as normal. She'd never been somewhere where she had to worry about jet lag. And yet, as Hope was asleep in the car seat next to her, she knew it was likely to be an issue over the next few days.

'I feel like I could go back to bed, but I'm not sure that's the most sensible idea,' she replied honestly.

'Well, don't feel under any pressure with us. If you want to sleep for the whole week, then you do that, honey. You do whatever makes you happy.'

Holly smiled gratefully as she turned and looked at Ben. Other than the interjection where he had replied to Anne, he had been silent the entire journey from the airport. Even after Holly had told Hope about Evan, he hadn't said a word. She knew part of it was to give her space. In being silent, he was probably hoping she could forget he was even there. But it felt like cowardice, like he had forced her into a corner and was now letting her deal with the repercussions.

'Is there anything you want to do while you're here, Ben?' Holly said, feeling the need to start up a conversation before the silence carried on any longer. 'I mean, you're in America, but you don't have to stay with me the whole time. If there's anywhere you want to go, I'm sure you can get a flight, right? Maybe you could spend a couple of days in New York or Vegas if you fancy?'

'I'm not sure that the ex-bank manager in Vegas would be a great idea,' Ben said. 'But no, I'm fine. I'm fine staying with Hope. And you, of course.'

Holly knew there was no point arguing, but hopefully, maybe after a couple of days of Ben seeing that she was absolutely fine, he might give her a little space. If not, this trip could end up feeling far, far longer than just one week.

32

The moment they stepped in through the front door, Hope was once again awake, and Jonathan ready to take charge of her.

'Come on you,' he said, his focus solely on his granddaughter. 'You and I have got a lot of catching up to do. Now, I found some teddies in one of the boxes in the playroom. Do you like teddies? Do you want to come and have a look at them with Grandad while your mummy and daddy take their things upstairs?'

'Teddies for Hope?' Hope asked, her eyes wide.

'Oh yes, all the teddies are for Hope,' Jonathan said, taking her by the hand and leading her through the house.

For a second, Holly watched them go before turning to Anne.

'It reminds me of when Evan first met her,' she said, unable to ignore the similarities between the father and son's first meetings with Hope. 'Did you know he bought her an obscene number of cuddly bunny rabbits?'

'Oh, I remember that,' Anne said with a sad laugh. 'Those are the ones she got stuck down the toilet, right?'

'Yes, those are the ones.'

So much time had passed, and those bunnies were still firm

favourites with Hope. Holly had even packed three in the suitcase and another had come in the hand luggage. Hope didn't like to be without her bunnies, and Holly had the feeling that would never change. Especially not now.

With a peculiar weight in her chest, Holly was still listening to Hope gabbling away to her grandfather when another yawn struck. It was only midday local time, but she didn't even know what that meant in the UK. All she knew was that she felt like she could sleep for a week. Of course, she had no intention of doing so. There were too many things to see and do.

'Honestly, I probably just need a coffee,' Holly said. Only as she finished her sentence, yet another yawn took over, this one so long, it made her jaw click.

'Oh, sweetie,' Anne said. 'You should go upstairs and get yourself some sleep. We'll be fine with the little one.'

This time, Holly actually considered the offer. Perhaps a quick nap would be a good idea in the long run, she thought, but she wasn't the only one who had had a long day. Not wanting to answer straight away, she looked to Ben.

'Hope's going to be overly tired, you know,' she said, not wanting to put on him too much already. After all, he had been travelling just as much as she had. 'She'll probably start kicking off any minute.'

'That's fine. I'll look after her,' Ben said. 'It's why I'm here.'

Holly looked back to Anne. 'In that case, thank you. If you could lead me to where Hope and I will be sleeping, that would be amazing.'

She moved to pick up the suitcase, but Ben got their first.

'Let me carry the bags up with you,' he said, 'then I can take a couple of things down to Hope to make sure she stays occupied.'

Whilst the outside of the house had been nothing like Holly had imagined, the inside had all the grand opulence that television and films had led her to believe about American homes. The staircase was wide and branched out at the top, while large windows showing woodland scenes behind the house looked like oil paintings. At a guess, there were probably five or six bedrooms, and Holly suspected most of them, if not all, had en-suites, too.

'Ben, you know the girls are coming to stay, for a bit at least,' Anne said, when they reached the landing. 'And we thought that it's probably easier if they take their own room. You know, with Catherine and Mel bringing the kids and everything. And Erin always stays in her and Em's room. She won't let me change it. Say if there's a problem, but Jonathan and I were thinking you could stay in his office. There's a pull-out sofa. It's comfy, but if you have a—'

'That's fine. A sofa will be absolutely fine,' Ben said.

A look of relief washed over Anne's face.

'Thank you. And it really is comfortable. I'm not ashamed to say that Jonathan has spent more than one night on there over the years.'

Normally, intrigue would have got the better of Holly, and she would have at least wondered why, but at that moment, her mind was on another track. If all the girls were sleeping in their normal rooms, and Anne and Jonathan were undoubtedly having theirs, then what space did that leave for her and Hope?

With a bolt of nausea, Holly looked at the door in front of her, and realised exactly whose bedroom she was going to be sleeping in.

33

Anne hovered outside the door. She reached for the handle, but she didn't open it. Not straight away.

'I think I just heard Hope call,' Ben said suddenly. 'I should check.'

Holly nodded. There was no need for her to reply. It had been so silent that they would have heard a pin drop. They all knew Ben was just using Hope as a reason to slip out of the situation, and Holly was grateful for that. She didn't need him there right now. She didn't want him there.

Only when his footsteps disappeared downstairs did Anne speak again.

'Will it be a problem?' she said, with no need to clarify what she was talking about. 'I'm happy to sleep here if you'd rather. From what Jonathan said, Erin has crashed out in here for a couple of nights already. It made her feel closer to him, I think.'

Holly didn't reply. She wasn't sure how to. She had wanted to feel closer to Evan. That had been the entire point of this trip. But to sleep in his childhood bedroom? She wasn't sure that was something she could do.

'Why don't you have a look and see how you feel?' Anne said.

Holly nodded. Still not yet able to find her voice.

Anne pushed open the door, yet rather than stepping inside, or making room for Holly to, she stood there for a moment, gazing at the space, as if she were absorbing all the memories that it held. When she turned back around and looked at Holly, there was a shimmer of tears in her eyes.

'You know, he told me off for changing it,' she said quietly, stepping in and allowing Holly to see the neutral space beyond. It didn't look like a young boy's bedroom. Or even a lived-in bedroom. It was very much a stylish guest room, with muted bedsheets, numerous cushions and even a comfy-looking, white, wicker chair. 'He was joking, of course,' Anne continued. 'But he said that me renovating the room was basically forgetting he existed. And it wasn't like that. Of course, it wasn't. He always still stayed in here when he visited. But now, I wish I'd kept it the same, you know, just for a little longer. Maybe so you and Hope could have seen.'

Anne sniffed deeply before shaking her head, as if she could shake the thoughts from her mind that easily. Then, after a pause, she turned around to look at Holly and when she spoke again, her tone was far more jovial.

'He wouldn't want us to have stayed stuck in the past,' Anne said. 'He wouldn't have wanted that for any of us. This is what he would have wanted. You, here in a nice space. I'm sure he'd have thought of nothing worse than some dated shrine full of childhood certificates and trophies.'

'I'm sure you're right,' Holly said, finally finding her voice again, although she couldn't help but think of those trophies. She couldn't even imagine what they would have been for. Maybe if Anne still had them in the loft or somewhere, she could have a look through them.

A heartbeat of silence followed before Anne fixed a smile on her face.

'Well, I should go and see how Jonathan's doing with Hope. I'm sure it's time she had a little snack. And him too, for that matter. He can get terribly hangry.'

Holly nodded. She knew she was meant to smile at Anne's attempt at a joke, but she couldn't find it in her. Still, before Anne could go, Holly reached forward, wrapped her arms around her not-quite-mother-in-law, and squeezed her tightly. For a moment, the two of them remained there, holding one another. Two women both lacking the words for their loss. When they finally broke apart, Holly wiped the tears from her eyes.

'Thank you. Thank you for this,' she said.

34

Holly had thought it would be impossible to fall asleep. What, with all the thoughts whirling around her mind, from the worry of Hope adjusting to the new time zone, to the excitement of what the next few days sightseeing could contain. And yet, her head had barely touched the pillow when she fell asleep and it was, by all accounts, the deepest sleep she had had since Evan's death. It was as if her body didn't want to wake up; it just wanted to stay where it was, not having to think about the present or the future. She probably could have stayed asleep for several hours longer had a loud thud not woken her up.

Sitting up, Holly took a moment to gather her bearings. The day came back to her. The flight and the travel and even the room she was sleeping in. The word 'trophies' flitted back into her head, but before she could think why, there was yet another thud. Rolling herself off the bed, Holly headed out into the corridor.

'I'm ever so sorry. Did we wake you?' Anne said. She had changed since the aeroplane, and probably had a shower too, judging by her clean hair and made-up face. She looked fabulous. A far cry from the woman Holly had first met three days ago. 'I just thought that while I had Ben here, I would put him to use, get down a couple of boxes from the loft. I'm sorry if we woke you.'

'No, no, it's fine, it's fine,' Holly assured her. She looked to where Ben was currently climbing down the loft ladder. 'How long have I been asleep?'

When Ben reached the floor, he glanced at his watch.

'Not that long. Two and a half hours? Hope's gone to sleep now. God, she fought it. You know what she gets like when she's overly tired. We didn't want to disturb you, so we put up a cot in Anne and Jonathan's room. I thought I'd let her have an hour or so. That way, she should still go to sleep at an okay time.'

'We just put the cot there while you were asleep,' Anne said, clearly worried about offending Holly. 'We'll move it into your room as soon as she's awake.'

Holly nodded. 'It's fine. It was a sensible thing to do.'

For a second, Holly thought a silence was about to form, but before it could, Anne was speaking again.

'Well, we were just going to go downstairs and have a look at some of these things if you want to join us? I bet there are some things in there that will make you chuckle.'

This chirpy, bright-eyed woman was the one Holly had spoken to so many times and yet something about her felt odd. Probably it was because Holly knew Anne's happiness had to be a pretence. Or maybe Anne was just like Holly and knew that crying wouldn't help matters. In fact, Holly couldn't even remember the last time she'd cried about Evan. Was that strange? Probably not. Despite the obvious tragedy, there was still plenty to keep her busy and be grateful for.

'I was going to put the kettle on too and maybe have a slice of pie,' Anne added. 'I'm sure you must be starving. The rest of us ate while you were asleep. I can fix you something when we get downstairs.'

Holly hesitated as her eyes shifted from Anne to Ben, or more precisely, the item in Ben's arms. She didn't doubt that it was stuffed full of Evan memorabilia. Anne had said before that most of the photo albums were in the loft and there could well be some of those intriguing trophies she'd mentioned too, but as Holly thought about what the box held, a deep-rooted heat began to burn in her chest.

'Do you mind if I don't, actually? It's just, I thought maybe I'd go for a walk. It's going to be dark early, right? I thought I'd like to see a bit of the area before night-time.'

Holly could see the disappointment flash in Anne's eyes and she was about to backtrack on her comment, but before she could, Anne was smiling broadly.

'Of course, yes, of course. You don't want to be cramped in a house after all those hours on the plane. Silly me. No, you're right. A walk will probably do you good. And it's ever so pretty. Cold, though. You'll need your gloves and hat for sure.'

'Where is it you want to go?' Ben said, still holding the box. 'I'll come with you. As long as you're all right to wake up Holly, Anne?'

'Well...' Anne went to speak, but Holly looked at her with desperation in her eyes.

Holly didn't want to refuse Ben's offer. Not when he was trying to help. But she was already finding his presence a little suffocating.

Thankfully, her not-quite-mother-in-law knew exactly what Holly's look meant.

'Holly will be fine, Ben,' Anne said with a wave of her hand. 'Honestly, it's ever such an easy walk to the lake. Down the driveway, turn right and keep walking until you see it straight ahead of you. Assuming that you want to go to the lake, that is?' Anne paused, her expression changing.

'The lake sounds perfect,' Holly said, knowing there was no

other answer she could give that wouldn't cause Anne a lasting bout of guilt. Besides, what was Holly meant to do? Avoid every place with a lake, or sea, or deep river for the rest of her life? No, she couldn't do that. The sooner she got past all of this, the better. 'I won't be long. I just want to get my bearings. I'll be back long before it's dark.'

As she finished speaking, Ben inhaled sharply. Holly was certain he was going to object. That was probably what he wanted to do. Instead, what he said was, 'Just make sure you wrap up warm, okay?'

A smile sparked in Holly. Her American adventure was about to begin.

35

Anne was right about Holly needing a hat and gloves. Even with them, and her thickest coat on, the cold was still biting. It was only when she reached the end of the driveway that she realised she hadn't yet had a shower or bath. All that time travelling, and Holly hadn't even changed her clothes before falling asleep. She would need to do that as soon as she got back, or Evan's family would start worrying about her personal hygiene.

But for now, she wanted to focus only on the moment.

Despite all the images Holly had created in her mind of the place where Evan had grown up, and the picture he'd tried to paint of the scenery and landscape, she now knew she had got it so wrong. Holly had imagined him cycling his bike down wide pavements, past brand-new trucks. She'd envisioned mums with pushchairs sipping on takeaway coffees and groups of joggers oblivious to the world as they sped past with their earbuds in. She hadn't imagined his childhood surrounded by trees, his bike bumping and skidding on rocks and potholes. So many times when he'd spoken to her, Evan had made out like the English countryside was the wildest, most expansive land of green he'd ever known, but that obviously wasn't the case. Here, untamed forests stretched as far as she could see.

As Holly carried on the road towards the lake, she remembered how Evan had once commented that one thing he loved most about walking in the UK was the pubs and how you never had to go that far without seeing one. Now she understood why he'd said that. She'd already been walking for fifteen minutes and the forest was showing no signs of thinning. Anne's idea of a very quick walk was further than Holly had anticipated, but that probably happened when you were living in a country as big as America.

Not wanting to get sucked into memories, Holly focused on the things around her. The birds that were different to those she saw at home, houses built in a way she'd never seen. She got her phone out and started snapping. She wanted to make sure that when she got home, she had plenty of photos to show everyone. No one would believe how incredible it all was otherwise.

After a leisurely twenty-five minutes walk, several buildings came into view, including a café. Then, as Holly looked out in front of her, she saw it.

How Ben or Anne could have worried she might be upset by the sight was beyond her. This was so, so different to home. To the Lake District. To anything else Holly had ever seen. And yet at the same time, it made sense why Evan would want to propose to her by the water. If you grew up next to a sight like this, Holly thought, it was a miracle you ever moved away. But then lots of people probably said the same about the Cotswolds and had she not split up with Dan all those years ago, and taken over the sweet shop, Holly knew she probably would have stayed in London her entire life.

The sky was the palest of blues, bordering on grey, although it remained cloudless. The crisp, cold air was the type you only got on a clear day. While the land was surprisingly flat, a few gentle slopes lined with fir trees rolled down to the water's edge, where gentle ripples glinted with yellow light.

As Holly sat down on the shingled beach area, she drew in a long breath and closed her eyes. The cold didn't seem so bad now, the breeze from the water, somehow warming. Evan had sat on this same beach, probably hundreds of times, and with her eyes shut like this, Holly could almost imagine he was there with her now. His fingertips resting on the stones, only millimetres from her own. His feet stretched forward as he lifted his eyes to the sky. That was the image that Holly held in her mind. The vision she wanted to hold on to forever. And perhaps she would have managed had a loud scream not broken her daydream.

36

Holly's eyes snapped open and she jumped to her feet. She turned from left to right, searching for the source of the sound. It took her only a moment to find it.

A young boy, perhaps five or six, was standing in the lake, with the freezing water already up to his thighs.

It was an instant reaction. A flood of adrenaline, fear and pain coursed through her. He was going to go deeper. He was going to go deeper and she wouldn't be able to reach him in time. Before she knew what she was doing, she was running along the shingle towards the child.

'Get him out! Get him out!' she yelled.

Holly's heart pounded as he forced her legs to run faster than they had ever done before. She could see the boy's mother just standing there, watching him go deeper and deeper. Did she not know how cold it was? How dangerous it was? It didn't matter if the boy was a good swimmer. It wouldn't be enough.

Holly was running in the lake now. The freezing water splashing up over her trousers, soaking her shoes and socks, just like it had done in the Lake District, less than a week ago. She couldn't let the same thing happen to this child as happened to Evan. She couldn't.

'What are you doing!' Holly yelled at the mother. 'Get him out of there, get him out!'

She ran to the boy, although he was moving now, towards the shore. Only a week ago, Holly would have assumed that getting back to the shore was enough. But Evan had got back to the shore. It hadn't been enough for him.

By the time Holly reached the boy, he was with his mother, who had lifted him up and was holding him on her hips.

Holly was breathless. The effort of the run and the surge of adrenaline had her heart racing. She doubled over with her hands on her knees as she panted, trying to catch some air. The child might be safe now, but the woman needed to know. She needed to know how reckless she had been with her son's life. And Holly was about to tell her as much when the woman started yelling.

'What the heck are you doing?' the mother shouted, her face only inches from Holly's. 'Who the hell do you think you are? Yelling at my boy like that? What's wrong with you, lady? Are you crazy?'

Holly opened her mouth, gawping like a fish. 'The cold water... It can... It's... It's...' She stopped, unable to get any further in the sentence.

As she stood there, her breaths still heaving, Holly's eyes went to the boy's clothes. He was dressed warmly in thick, green tracksuit bottoms, with matching green wellington boots. Though it wasn't the colour of his trousers that held Holly's attention, but the fact that they were entirely dry. Holly stared at the garment, trying to see if she was mistaken, only to know she wasn't. Other than his wellington boots, everything on the boy was bone-dry. But how could that have been, when she was so sure that the water had been up to his thighs? Only it hadn't been, she realised, her heart now skipping in her chest. That was what she'd thought she'd seen: a boy in danger. A boy about to follow the same fate as Evan. But it had never been the case. This boy had been completely fine, splashing in the shallow water in his wellington boots, with his mother watching on the entire time.

'I'm sorry,' Holly said, feeling the heat of tears prick her eyes. 'It's just my boyfriend... the water... a lake...'

She could no longer restrain her tears. They were streaming were down her cheeks, and she knew she looked ridiculous. No, worse, she looked insane. Was that it? Was she destined to fill the role of crazy widow? Forever seeing danger where there wasn't any?

'I'm so, so sorry,' she said again, before twisting away and preparing to leave, when the mother grabbed her arm. When Holly turned back, all the anger had gone from the woman's face and had been replaced by pure sadness.

'Holly?' she said, her voice near breathless. 'I can't believe it. Holly. It's you, isn't it?'

37

Holly stared at this woman, with dark, almond eyes that were all too familiar. She was older than Holly, probably in her late thirties, and her hair was hidden beneath a woolly bobble hat, but Holly knew it was curly, just like she knew that the boy in the woman's arms was actually only five, and his name was Parker.

'Catherine,' Holly said, realising she was looking at Evan's oldest sister. 'I'm so sorry. I didn't mean to scare him, I didn't mean... Parker?'

Holly looked at the little boy, who was now frowning with confusion at her. How she hadn't spotted it was Parker until now was a mystery to her. She had photos of him all around her house. From his first birthday, where he dressed up as a dinosaur, to his youngest cousin's christening, where he wore a mini suit, complete with bow tie. Holly even had the Christmas cards Catherine had sent both this year, and the year before, which also featured his older sister, Lily.

'There's no need to be silly, Park,' Catherine said, putting him back down on the shingle. 'This is Aunty Holly. You know Aunty

Holly. You've spoken to her on the computer. She's Uncle Evan's...
Uncle Evan's...'

Catherine let her sentence fade into the air, and Holly couldn't
blame her. She didn't know how to finish it either.

With a quick sniff, Catherine's cheeks rose into a smile.

'I told Mum and Dad I would be there an hour ago,' she said.
'But as she's already going to be cross with me for being late and
it's freezing out here; what do you say we go get a drink together?
There's a coffee shop around the corner.'

Holly didn't want to upset Anne. Not after everything she had
done for her. But she wasn't ready to go back to the house yet and
certainly not if all Evan's sisters had arrived. She would much
rather have a chance to talk to Catherine one on one, somewhere
quiet, before she had to face everyone. One sister at a time felt like
more than enough for her to handle.

'A coffee sounds great,' Holly agreed.

38

As they walked across the water's edge towards the coffee shop, Catherine messaged Anne to say she'd found Holly at the lake, and not to worry if she was back a little late as they were going for a drink and a quick catch-up. That had been the plan at least, although as soon as the pair had their drinks and sat down at a table, both of them seemed to struggle for words.

'How was the flight?'

'I'm sorry again about Parker.'

The pair spoke in unison, and Holly felt her cheeks colour.

'I'm sorry,' she said. 'You go.'

'No, no. It's fine,' Catherine replied. 'And I understand. I do. Parker in the water. It must have... I can imagine it was...'

So many half sentences. Holly wondered if this was what it was going to be like forever. People not knowing what they should say to her. Not being able to mention Evan's name. Was she giving the impression that she couldn't cope with hearing it? She hoped not. After all, the very reason she had come there was to learn more about Evan. For that to happen, people needed to realise she was completely fine talking about him.

'I came down here to feel close to him,' Catherine said, finally managing a complete sentence. 'I always think of him when I'm down here. We used to come a lot as kids. And teenagers, too. I was meant to go straight to Mum and Dad's. All the girls are coming over. I don't know if Mum told you that?'

Holly shook her head. 'No, but I was asleep most of the afternoon, and then I just needed to get out of the house.'

'I get it,' Catherine said. 'If things get too much, you need to say so, okay? Mum's not good with silence. She doesn't get that sometimes people need that.'

By people, Holly assumed Catherine was talking about herself. Parker was playing on a tablet, completely content with his game and the large chocolate chip cookie in front of him.

For a moment, neither of the women said anything.

'Where's Lily?'

'He saved the boy, right?'

They did it again. Spoke at exactly the same time. In another situation, it might even have been humorous, but it wasn't then. Rather than apologising or asking her question for a second time, Holly stayed silent and waited for Catherine to speak again. It didn't take long.

'Lily's with Blake,' Catherine said, not needing to clarify that this was her ex-husband. 'We didn't want to disrupt her too much. She's still got a couple of weeks of school left until winter break. We wanted to keep life as normal as possible for her, you know?'

Holly fully understood the decision and, for a split second, felt a flicker of guilt at dragging Hope halfway across the world. But then, Hope's life would never be normal again. Not with Evan gone.

Holly didn't say any more about the situation with Lily. She knew Catherine had gone through a divorce a year ago, and so shifting any attention back to the ex, Blake, didn't seem like something she would be grateful for. Which meant Holly knew exactly what Catherine was going to ask next. And all she could do was wait.

Silence began to settle before Catherine spoke again, far more quietly.

'He saved a boy, didn't he?' she said, with a slight warble. 'That was what Fin said. That it was icy, and a boy was messing around, and Evan saved him?'

A lump formed in Holly's throat as she thought of that moment for what had to be the thousandth time. She hadn't known. Even as Evan had raced out onto the ice, she hadn't even thought about what could have happened. Why hadn't she thought about that? Why hadn't she stopped him? With a firm sniff, she picked up her drink and sipped on it for long enough to abate the tears.

'He did. I don't know. He mustn't have known...'

'He knew,' Catherine said, with a forcefulness to her tone. 'Evan was such a strong swimmer, and he knew the water. He grew up here. He must have known. Going into the water in that weather... He must have known.'

'I don't think he realised how far out the boy was. And the ice... The ice...' Holly was back to talking in snippets again, although Catherine had found her voice.

'No. He grew up here. We spent winters on the lake. Winters where the lake froze over, too. Mum and Dad, they drilled it into him. Into all of us. He knew what would happen. He knew that going out in that water would have—'

'Stop it!' Holly didn't mean to shout. She hadn't even wanted to speak, but she couldn't let Catherine carry on. She couldn't. Because if what Catherine was saying was true, then Evan had gone into that water, knowing he was stripping Holly of a future with him and she couldn't believe that. She refused to.

'I'm sorry. I'm sorry, it's just... it's just...'

'No, I understand. I do, I'm sorry. I shouldn't have said anything.' Catherine looked for a moment as if she was going to reach across and take Holly's hand, but instead she sat back and picked up her coffee. 'We should probably get back to the house. Mum will be starting to worry.'

39

Back at the house, Holly headed straight to the shower. Catherine had driven her back from the lake, and apparently, Melissa was already there. The other sisters were expected imminently, she learned, and the last thing Holly wanted was to meet them looking as distressed and dishevelled as she felt.

When she was washed and dressed and feeling moderately more presentable, Holly sought out Ben and Hope.

'She would have slept for hours,' Ben said, as Holly bent down and pulled Hope in for a tight hug. 'She didn't want to wake up, but I didn't think it was a good idea to let her sleep for any longer. I was worried she'd just end up waking in the middle of the night.'

The completely glazed look in Hope's eyes confirmed everything Ben had just said. Normally, Hope would wake up from a nap full of energy and raring to go, but she looked like she could fall back asleep at any moment. She was already snuggling back into Holly, like she was trying to find a comfortable enough position to do so.

'Are you tired, Hopey?' Holly said, kissing her daughter on the top of her head. 'Don't worry, we'll get an early night tonight, okay?'

Hope nodded, still not managing to talk through the drowsiness. Instead, it was Ben who replied.

'Talking of early nights,' he said. 'I thought we could put her cot downstairs in the office with me.'

Holly frowned. 'Why?'

'You know, just so you get a little space.'

Holly shook her head. 'I don't need space. I need Hope. There's plenty of room for a cot in my room. Or she can sleep in bed with me. You know she likes to do that when she's tired.'

'I know, it's not a case of room. I just thought that—'

'Well, don't,' Holly said. 'Don't think about it. If I'd had my way, it would be me and Hope here on our own.'

'Holly—'

'No, Ben. I get you think that you're doing me a favour, but Hope and I have to get used to this. We have to get used to a life without Evan. You can't be there, waiting at every turn. It doesn't help anyone. Not in the long run. Having you here, trying to do every little thing for me so I don't have to lift a finger isn't real life. At some point, we're going to have to face the fact that when we go home to England, and everyone goes back to their normal life, Hope and I are going to be on our own.'

'Mamma?'

It was the first thing Hope had said since Holly got back, and Holly was about to ask her daughter if she needed anything, but when she looked down, Holly realised that Hope had just been there, listening to the way she'd spoken to Ben.

Holly never spoke to him like that normally, and would never dream of doing it in front of Hope, but as a sudden pressure constricted around her chest, Holly realised there was something worse than how she had spoken, and that was the words she had said. Words she knew Hope had understood.

With her eyes glazed with tears, Hope's bottom lip trembled as she stared up at Holly.

'Hope on her own?' she said. 'Hope don't want own. Hope doesn't want to be on own.'

40

Holly was making a mess of things; she knew that. She knew Ben was only trying to help, and hiding the truth from Hope, even though it had only been for a few days, was only making this time now even harder. But this, speaking like that in front of Hope, was the biggest mess-up she had made so far.

'Hope, come downstairs with Daddy,' Ben said, reaching down to take Hope's hand, but Holly pushed it out of the way.

'No, it's fine. Hopey, it's fine. I'm sorry, Mummy didn't mean to speak like that. She didn't. You won't ever be on your own. Okay? You and I won't ever be on our own. We have Daddy, and Georgia. And Nanny and Grandad.'

'Lots of nannies and grandads,' Hope answered, still sniffing.

'Yes, you're right,' Holly said, pulling back the tears. Crying would make Hope think there was something wrong, and right now, that was the last thing she wanted. Fighting against the pain in her chest, she forced her face into a bright, happy smile. 'And we have Aunty Jamie and Uncle Fin. And Aunty Caroline.'

'And Uncle Giles,' Hope added.

'Yes, and Uncle Giles,' Holly agreed. 'We have all these people in our lives. We're never going to be alone, you understand?'

Hope nodded, and for a split second, Holly thought that would be the end of the matter, but then Hope spoke again.

'Evvy on his own?' she said, her intonation all that was needed to pose the question. 'Where's Evvy?'

Holly didn't have a reply. She could feel Ben twitching beside her, wanting to scoop Hope away and probably explain things a thousand times better than she was managing. But Holly couldn't let him do that. She couldn't let him take this part of Evan from her.

'Evvy's not on his own,' she said, not sure how she was going to carry on. 'He's with his grandma and grandad.'

'He is?' Hope said, her eyes widening.

'He is. I promise you he's okay. He's okay, and we're okay, all right? But...' Holly thought she might as well use the moment of having Hope's attention to ensure Ben didn't get his way when the evening came. 'Do you think you'd be okay to sleep in Mummy's room with her tonight? Would that be okay?'

Hope nodded eagerly. 'Hope sleep in Mummy's bed?'

'Of course you can.' Holly let out a light chuckle as she picked up her daughter. The guilt from her words still sat there like a dull ache in her chest.

They were still standing like that, at the top of the stairs, Ben watching over the pair as Holly squeezed Hope as tightly as she could, when the doorbell rang. A moment later, Anne's voice called out.

'Jonathan, the rest of the girls are here,' she said.

Holly was sure Evan's mother had spoken at such a volume so Holly could hear. Letting go of Hope, she stood up and smiled at her daughter.

'I guess it's time for you and me to meet your au—' The first syllable left her mouth before Holly could stop it, but she couldn't finish the word. It was one word, and yet it stung the back of her throat, because it wasn't really true. They weren't Hope's aunties. Not now. And they never would be. Still, Holly fixed the smile back on her face and prayed she had been quick enough that Hope didn't notice.

'Let's go meet Evvy's sisters, shall we?' she said instead.

41

As Holly moved to go down the stairs, Ben cleared his throat.

'Holly?'

'Don't,' she said. She didn't know what Ben was about to say, but she was certain she didn't want to hear it. 'I can't. Not right now. This is important. Meeting Evan's sisters is important.'

'I know it is,' he said, his voice soft. 'It's incredibly important for you. And Hope too. Which is why I'm heading out. Jonathan's going to drop me at the mall and give you two a chance to meet everyone. As much as you might believe otherwise, I do know that you need some space.'

Yet another surge of guilt rolled through Holly. It was strange, she thought. The last thing she'd expected to feel after she lost the love of her life was guilt, and yet it was currently her most common emotion. As such, for a split second, she was about to tell Ben that he didn't need to leave. He had travelled all this way to be here for her, and the last thing she wanted was to add to her feelings of guilt because she was worried about him being on his own. But before she could respond, she changed her mind again. Ben leaving for a couple of hours was probably the most sensible thing he could do. She didn't want him to feel like he had to hide away in some corner, but at the same time, she didn't want to have to deal with introductions and explanations as to who he was and why he was there.

'Thank you,' she said.

Ben nodded. 'It's not that far away and Ubers are everywhere, apparently. So if you need me, just call, okay? I'll come straight back.'

'Ben Thornbury getting an Uber for me. This must be serious,' Holly joked, although Ben's face remained completely impassive.

'Just take care of yourself, okay? And remember, they're all hurting. People can say things they don't mean when they're hurting.'

Ben's last words lingered in Holly's mind. Was he talking about her? That seemed the most obvious assumption, and yet before she could comment, Jonathan was standing with his coat on, looking up at them.

'You ready to go, buddy?' he said.

'Sure,' Ben replied. 'Thank you again for driving me there.'

'No worries.'

Ben leaned down and kissed Hope on the top of the head, before repeating the action on Holly. Then, without another word, he headed down the stairs and out the front door with Jonathan. With a deep breath in, Holly looked at Hope and tried to stop the trembling that had started in her hand.

'Well, baby girl,' she said, her nerves rising with every passing moment, 'I guess it's time we meet the family.'

42

There were four women waiting in the kitchen when Holly came downstairs with Hope. Holly immediately knew which sisters were missing: Evan's triplets. A flash of gratitude flooded her. As it was, facing three sisters at once was a daunting task and Holly's pulse had only proceeded to rise since seeing them. She couldn't imagine how much worse it would have been if there were another two there.

'Holly, darling. Come, let me make you a drink,' Anne said. 'And you girls can have a chat.'

Evan had adored his sisters, even though they'd driven him mad, each in different ways. Catherine was the oldest and, from what he'd said, the one who like to take charge. Or the 'bossy one', as he sometimes referred to her. Holly could tell that Catherine liked to be in control of things, and she didn't back down easily, but was that because she was bossy or because she had five younger siblings that she'd probably had to be in charge of at one time or another?

His other two older sisters were Mel and Ashley. Ashley was the one sister Holly had met in person when she came and visited the villa in France. But despite that week, where they had really bonded, Holly had spoken to her far less on video calls than the other sisters. Ashley worked for an NGO that sent her to all different countries around Asia, so her time difference was even more difficult to get to grips with than the rest of Evan's family. As such, Evan tended to speak to her when he was travelling. It was only by chance that she was back in America. Only by chance that she was there to be with the rest of her family in their mourning.

'I'm so sorry, Holly,' Ashley said, pulling Holly straight in for a hug. 'I can't imagine what you're going through. Thank you. Thank you for coming over with Mum. For what it's worth, I think you're definitely doing the right thing. You don't need to be at home right now. You can't do anything. I feel like you being here is what Evan would have wanted you to do. But then I guess you already know that, right?'

Holly smiled gratefully. It was a thought that she'd had, too. How happy Evan would be to know that his family was playing a part in her healing. If that's what she was doing? Whether this was how people were meant to get over loss, she wasn't sure, but she certainly felt like it was a good step forward, taking a proactive approach, rather than sitting at home and sobbing all day.

'Hey, Holly. Hey, Hope.' The next sister dropped to the ground, offering Hope her first hug, before she stood back up and embraced Holly. Holly didn't need to ask what her name was. Only one of Evan's sisters had bright-red hair, and that was Mel. Despite not having met in person, they had spoken dozens of times on video calls before, though normally, Hope took charge of those.

'I hope the flight was okay,' Mel continued as she stood up. 'Mum said you're exhausted. It makes sense.'

'I'm pretty shattered,' Holly admitted. 'Although I think Hope's even worse.'

'Poor thing. I don't know if it's any good, but I brought a load of clothes for Hope with me.' Mel gestured to the corner of the room, where several large carrier bags were stacked on a chair and filled to overflowing. 'Most of the things were Lauren's that she's grown out of now, but I've put a few of Donny's jumpers in there, too. I thought they might be useful. But please, just leave anything you don't want. Don't feel like you have to take anything if you don't want to.'

'Thank you, that's really kind,' Holly said.

'It's nothing. I mean, you flew all the way out here.'

Despite being younger than both Ashley and Catherine, Mel looked older. It was possibly something in the way she dressed, with her high-neck jumper and flat shoes, or the fact that she wore makeup far more similar to her mother than Ashley and Catherine, who were both bare-faced.

'We really appreciate you coming over, you know,' Catherine said, stepping in line next to her sister. 'I don't think I said that before.'

'We do,' Ashley agreed. 'It's really generous of you. After all, you were the one who knew him the best.'

At these words, two loud coughs cut through the air from the other side of the room, although it wasn't from one person. It was from two. Two individual people who had coughed at almost exactly the same moment.

Holly turned around, her heart now knocking against her ribcage. There, on the other side of the room, two tear-stained faces were glaring straight at her, and she knew without a doubt who she was looking at.

Evan's triplets.

43

When Evan had talked about Holly meeting his family, she had always embraced the idea with full enthusiasm and excitement. Almost...

She had loved meeting Ashley in France, and couldn't wait to meet Melissa and her children, given that there was less than a year between Hope and Melissa's youngest and Holly always got the impression that they would get on like a house on fire. She knew Catherine had been through a tough time with her divorce, but whenever Holly spoke to her on the computer, she had a smile on a face, and was talking about all the good things going on in her life, rather than the negatives. In Holly's mind, that was a testament to the type of person she was. And as for Anne and Jonathan, Holly had loved Evan's parents from the first time they spoke.

But as welcoming as his parents and elder sisters had been, Holly had always felt a sense of fear about meeting Evan's full family. Fear that came with the thought of meeting the other two triplets.

Of all his sisters, Evan had spoken about Erin and Emily the most, which wasn't really a surprise. They were triplets, and if the stories were true, they had been inseparable during their childhood.

They had shared a bedroom until the age of ten, when his parents had decided that Evan shouldn't have to share a room with his sisters any more. Most boys would have been happy with this, but Holly remembered Evan telling her how he'd felt like he was suddenly going to be left out of things and had hated going to sleep on his own. Even when he was fifteen, he would sometimes go into their room late at night just to talk and end up falling asleep in one of their beds.

They had been in classes together and had a crazy sense of competitiveness, despite their camaraderie. If one did better in a test one week, you could guarantee the others would work their socks off to make sure they beat them the next week.

They were best friends and had been since the day they were born, so it was no wonder Holly felt intimidated by that. But now... Now, what was there to be intimidated by? It didn't matter who knew him best. What mattered was the fact that they all loved him. They all loved him, and he was gone.

Holly stepped towards them, not sure if they were going to hug her or not, when one of them spoke.

'You should have stopped him from going in the water,' she said.

Holly paused and tilted her head to the side slightly, sure she couldn't have heard her properly.

'Sorry, I—'

'You should have stopped him from going in. If you'd have done that, he'd still be here now. This is on you. His death is on you.'

44

It felt like the air had been snatched from Holly's lungs. There was no mistaking what had been said. Evan's sister, one of the triplets, no less, one of the closest people in his entire world, blamed Holly for his death. And that wasn't the worst bit. The worst bit was that she was right.

Tears choked Holly's throat as she stepped forward, not sure what she was going to say. Silence had swallowed the room, every breath held, and then, before she could work out what she was going to do, the same triplet spoke again.

'Screw this. I'm not staying here pretending to be happy families with someone we don't even want here.'

With that, she swivelled on her heel and marched out of the room.

'Erin!' Anne called, rushing after her daughter. 'Come back here. Come back here now. You need to apologise.'

The silence threatened again, and Holly could feel a pressure building up around her heart space. It was like the absence of sound was an amplifier to the pain. That silence was the most unbearable since Evan's death, but what broke it was a thousand times worse.

'Mamma, why Nanny cross?'

Hope's voice caused Holly to gasp.

'Hope... Hope, I'm—' Holly tried, only to find herself struggling to catch her breath. She had brought Hope to America to protect her from hurt. To make this loss easier. Now she was witnessing yet another scene Holly should have sheltered her from.

'Hey, Hope,' Ashley said, stepping forward and crouching down by her. 'You remember me, right? Aunty Ashley? Do you want to come with me to the playroom?'

Ashley looked at Holly expectantly, as if waiting for her approval, but when Holly made no sound, Ashley moved in and took Hope's hand anyway.

'I'll come with you too,' Melissa said. 'Your cousin Lauren is really looking forward to meeting you, Hope. All your cousins are. And I should probably check how Tommy's doing looking after all the kids.'

It was the first time Holly realised Melissa's husband was visiting, too, but she still didn't say anything. Instead, she was standing in exactly the same place as she had been when Erin walked out of the room.

But it was the other triplet Holly was looking at now. Emily.

Holly's heart drummed in her chest as she waited. Waiting for Emily to say the same thing. To confirm what Erin had said, and how it was what all of them were thinking. Holly was to blame. That was what she expected Emily to say. Instead, the third triplet let out a long sigh.

'It's gonna take time, that's all. Everyone grieves differently, you know.'

Holly nodded, though she didn't know. Not really. This was

her first experience of grief, and until now, she had thought she was doing it all properly. She had carried on putting Hope first – or had tried to at least – and it wasn't like she was ignoring the issue that Evan was gone. The fact she had travelled halfway across the world to his childhood home was evidence enough of that, but now she suddenly had the feeling she was doing it all wrong.

'I'll go talk to her,' Emily said, breaking the silence that had once again settled. 'Mum tends to make things worse with Erin. But we'll talk later, okay?'

45

As Emily left after her sister, Holly didn't doubt her words about Anne making matters worse. The previously mild and good-humoured woman was yelling so loudly, Holly doubted there was a single person in the entire house that couldn't hear. It wouldn't have surprised Holly if they could hear her all the way down at the lake.

'She watched the man she loved die in front of her!' Anne was yelling. 'Can you imagine? And he was going to propose to her that day! Did he tell you that? Because he told me. Rang me that morning and said he was going to do it. Poor Holly had to be given the ring with his belongings. Can you imagine what that was like for her? Really, Erin, of all the things—'

'Please don't listen to Erin,' Catherine said softly, drawing Holly's focus away from Anne's voice. 'You know it's not true.'

With Emily gone, only Catherine and Holly remained. The kitchen which, only a few minutes ago, had been filled with people was now practically empty.

'Everything I told you at the café is true. You need to remember that. Not just because of Erin, but for yourself. I promise. Ask Ashley, ask Melissa. Ask Mum and Dad. I promise you. Evan knew the risks with what he was doing. You are not to blame.'

Holly nodded numbly.

'You will go down there this instant, or you will find yourself very unwelcome in this house—' Anne was still going, although once again, Holly was distracted from exactly what she was saying as Ashley and Melissa returned to the kitchen without Hope.

'I don't think any of us want to listen to that, do we?' Melissa said, closing the door behind her. 'Hope and Lauren are already best friends, and Tommy is in charge. Now, why don't I get us some food? The neighbours started filling the fridge the moment they heard what happened. I don't think there's any way we can get through it all, but we should at least give it a try.'

'Good thinking,' Catherine agreed, although Ashley cleared her throat, as if there was something different she had been expecting her sister to say. A slight pink coloured Melissa's cheek.

'Holly,' Melissa said tentatively. A churn of apprehension corkscrewed in Holly's stomach. 'I'm really sorry about what I said earlier.'

Earlier? What had Melissa said to her earlier? Holly wracked her brains, but came up with nothing. So far that day, she and Melissa had only shared a very brief conversation, in which Melissa had offered Hope a load of old clothes. The last thing Holly could imagine was that she was apologising about that. Unless she wanted to take them back.

Holly frowned, unsure of how to respond, though thankfully Melissa saw her confusion.

'About the cousins? I said to Hope about meeting her cousins, but I didn't check that you were still okay thinking about them like that. It was instinctive, you know? They all talk about their little cousin Hope, who lives with Uncle Evan in England. Lived.' She corrected herself.

Holly felt her lips stretch into a smile. 'No, it's fine. It's good,' she said. 'Evan would have wanted that. Evan did want that.'

'Good. That's good.'

Holly expected her words to elicit a smile or response from Melissa and the other sisters too, but instead, they were silent. Catherine had momentarily stopped pulling Pyrex dishes out of the fridge and was staring at Ashley and while no words were spoken, Holly knew they were exchanging a thought. Something they both wanted to say.

An unexpected twinge struck behind her ribs. If sisters could communicate like this, with a single glance conveying a thousand meanings, then how much closer was that bond for triplets? When Holly looked at things like that, it became even more obvious why Erin hated her.

She was about to say something to that effect when Ashley started speaking again.

'Holly, I know this probably isn't the best time, but there's something we want to ask you. And we hope it's okay.'

46

Holly was officially regretting her decision to make this trip. As far as she could tell, in twenty-four hours, she had been forced to tell Hope about Evan, terrorised Evan's nephew at the lake and caused a huge argument between Anne and one of her youngest. Whatever was going to come next, Holly didn't want to hear it. She didn't want to know. But there was nothing she could say to stop it from happening.

Evan's three older sisters were silent now as they stood there staring at Holly intently. From the way Catherine was biting down on her bottom lip and Mel was picking at her nails, Holly could tell that they were more than a little nervous about whatever they were going to say. And that was enough for Holly to regret her decision to come here even more.

Given that it was Ashley who had last spoken, and told Holly they wanted to ask her something, Holly assumed she would be the one to pose whatever this horrific question was. But when the sisters next spoke, it was Catherine who took the lead.

'I know you heard what Mum was yelling there, but she didn't need to say that to Erin. I don't mean she didn't need to yell,'

Catherine said, seeming notably less self-assured than normal. 'She absolutely did. Trust me, Erin's going to get an earful from the rest of us, too. But Mum didn't need to say that bit about the ring. Erin already knew. We all did. Evan told us the day he bought it.'

'Oh,' Holly said. She wasn't sure how this was supposed to make her feel. The way Ashley had spoken made it sound as if there was a question they wanted to ask. Not just some details about Evan they wanted to fill her in on. Not that Holly wasn't grateful for all the information she could garner. After all, that was the reason she had come to America.

'Yeah, we knew he was planning on proposing ages ago,' Ashley said, now joining in. 'He started sending us pictures of all these rings in the summer, asking our opinions on what sort of style you'd like. To be honest, I think he already knew what he was going to get you. He was just excited. He knew he'd found the person he wanted to spend the rest of his life with and wanted us all to know it. I think that's the only reason he was asking our opinions on the rings.'

Holly nodded. She wasn't entirely sure that was the right reaction, but then she didn't know what reaction she was meant to have. She didn't even know why they were bringing this up. Evan had been looking at rings as far back as the summer. Why hadn't he bought one then? She wanted to ask him. Why hadn't he bought one in the summer and proposed all those months ago? Then they would never have been in the Lake District in winter. Then he would never have gone into the icy water. Then he would have been the one to slip the ring on her finger as he knelt down on one knee, rather than her having to put it on herself in the passenger seat of Giles's car, less than twelve hours after Evan had died.

As she glanced down at her hand, Holly realised what the

issue was. She was wearing the ring. She was wearing the ring Evan hadn't actually given to her and the girls didn't like it. That's what they were about to tell her; she needed to take the ring off. Perhaps they even thought they had more right to it than she did. That was nonsense, of course. There was no way Holly was going to hand it over, but she knew what they wanted now, at least. She needed to stop wearing her ring while she was in this house.

A sad chuckle rose from her throat. It was yet another point to add to the ever-growing list of regrets she was building about this trip.

'The thing is,' Ashley said, 'we know he wanted to marry you. We know you two were the real deal. And I can't imagine what that's like for you, so we just wanted to ask if it's okay that we still refer to you as Evan's fiancée. And as our sister-in-law. I mean, I don't know how that works, you know, just...'

'Yes. Yes!' Holly said, one of the thousand cracks in her totally shattered heart healing by just a fraction. 'Thank you,' she said. 'Thank you, and I'm so, so sorry.'

'Shush, don't you dare apologise,' Catherine said, wafting the comment away. A moment later, her arms were wrapped around Holly and the other two sisters quickly joined in the embrace. For a minute, Holly remained there, wholly engulfed in her sisters-in-law's love.

When they broke away, Melissa smiled at her.

'And please ignore Erin,' she added. 'Honestly, she is taking it hard. We all are, but she'll come around, I promise. Evan loved you. That's enough for us. For all of us.'

47

It was women only sitting at the table. Ben was yet to return from the mall, while Tommy and Jonathan had opted to eat with the children in the play room. As such, it probably wrong for Holly to hope that dinner was going to be a happy event. After all, these women had all just lost their brother, but after the comment about being called Evan's fiancée, she had thought that there might be some more bonding. A chance to learn stories about Evan: what he was like as a child, various misdemeanours he got into. That type of thing. But every time someone started to speak, Erin almost always cut them off.

'Do you remember the time when—' Melissa started.

'Do we have to?' Erin said. Her mother had forced her down to the dining table like she was some unruly teenager, not an adult, and she had come begrudgingly and slumped down in a chair. As lovely as the food was, none of them were really in the mood for eating, but while the rest of them slowly picked away, trying to give an impression of enjoying the meal, Erin simply glared at everyone, and Holly couldn't help but feel she got the brunt of the scowls. As for the food, Erin's knife and fork remained pristinely clean on the table beside her empty plate. She wasn't even trying to pretend.

Ashley glowered at her younger sister. Holly didn't know what Mel had been about to say, but she was sure it was something she wanted to hear.

'You're not the gatekeeper here, Erin,' Ashley said. 'We want to talk about Evan.'

'Really?' Erin said, a small smirk twisted on the corner of her lips. 'Do you want to talk about the fact that as soon as he met Holly, he stopped coming back to see us? That she basically cut him out of our lives?'

'Erin!' Anne covered her mouth in shock as she looked at Holly. 'I'm so sorry, Holly,' she said.

Holly opened her mouth, not entirely sure what she was going to say, but she didn't get a chance. Erin had no intention of stopping.

'Well, it's true. You know it is. He used to come back four times a year, before her. And we saw him once last Christmas. That was it. He practically forgot about us. We all know he wasn't even going to come home this year. He expected Mum and Dad to fly all that way instead.'

Holly was flabbergasted. Evan spoke about his family all the time. He had pictures of his sisters in his wallet, for crying out loud. How many guys did that? And he rang them at all hours. Not to mention invited them over to the UK and the house in France. Ashley had been the only one who came. And while he knew that Catherine and Mel had commitments with the children, and work played a part in restricting Emily's time away, Erin was an artist. She was the only one who had the freedom to come and see them whenever she wanted, and she had chosen not to.

'That's not true,' Emily said, for once standing up to her sister. 'You saw him three months ago when he was in New York.'

'For two hours!' Erin said emphatically. 'He used to stay for days when he came before. We'd go to shows, hang out. We'd catch up properly. When *she* came along, he just wanted to be on the next flight back to England.'

'That's what it's like when you've got a family,' Catherine tried.

'But they're not his family!' Ashley insisted. 'They're not. Hope's not his. For God's sake, she's brought the child's actual dad with her on this trip. Does no one else think that's odd? God, Holly, you must have thought you'd hit the jackpot when you found Evan. All the money you could ever want and you got to carry on with the other guy on the side. I just can't believe Evan was stupid enough to fall for someone like that.'

Holly felt her teeth grind together. She didn't want to get pulled into this. She didn't. Erin was Evan's sister, and she needed to grieve however was best for her. If attacking Holly was what Erin needed to do, Holly would try to stomach it the best she could. After all, the people at home knew the truth. Jamie, Fin. People who knew Evan knew how real their relationship was. Anne, who spoke to him every week, with Holly and Hope there on the phone too, knew all about their life. Erin was angry. Angry at this situation and Holly understood that. She wanted to respect that. But it was getting harder and harder with every spiteful word that came out of Erin's mouth.

Holly needed Erin to rein it in. She had said her piece. As long as she was done, Holly could hold it together. Only Erin wasn't done.

'I don't know why you all can't see that he somehow thought this façade meant more to him than his actual blood,' she spat. 'It was an embarrassment. The way he spoke about her and that kid, like it was his, was an embarrassment.'

That was a step too far.

Holly watched as hackles raised on every other person around the table, all of whom were ready to come to her defence. But Holly didn't need them to. She only had another five days to spend with this family, and there was no way she was going to let one of them make her feel unwelcome. Like Catherine and Ashley said, she was Evan's fiancée. She had a place at this table.

'How dare you…' The sympathy Holly had felt for Erin only a moment ago had transformed into outright fury. 'How dare you speak like that?'

And before she could stop herself, Holly felt every word she had kept trapped inside since meeting Evan's triplet spilling from her lips.

48

Holly was locked in a glaring match with Erin, and she had no intention of backing down. Perhaps earlier today, when the jet lag had been at its worst, she would have bowed her head and carried on chewing her food quietly. Perhaps if the other sisters hadn't taken her in, called her their sister-in-law and proved there were things that mattered in life more than paperwork and legalities, Holly would have been able to hold it in a little longer. But not now. Not after hearing the way Erin just spoke about Evan and Hope. Erin was supposed to love her brother and yet she was tarnishing his memory there in front of the people who mattered most to him in the entire world. Holly was only grateful that Hope was eating in the playroom with Jonathan, Tommy, and her cousins, so she didn't have to see the way she was about to erupt.

'He invited you over to England and to the villa,' Holly said. 'He invited every one of you repeatedly. Ashley is the only one who actually came. And he asked you all to come over for Christmas this year, too. He wanted the whole family there. We both did.'

Her words were true, but they weren't enough to make Erin back down.

'Oh, we were just supposed to drop everything and fly over there?'

'The way you wanted him to do when he came here, you mean? You have no idea how disappointed he was when everyone started cancelling coming to France last year. Ashley will tell you. He was so excited about a family get-together. But he didn't let you guys know that, of course, because he didn't want you to feel bad that you didn't come.'

'Flying the family over to France isn't exactly a cheap option, Holly,' Catherine said quietly.

Holly didn't want to ostracise Evan's eldest sister, not when she had done her best to make her feel so welcome. But she couldn't stand Erin holding the entire conversation hostage. She just hoped Catherine and the others would understand that. Particularly as she was nowhere near finished.

'You're right. But you know Evan would have paid. And I know you didn't want to use his money. I get that. I didn't either. If you want to go through my bank account and check that, go for it. Evan and I split things equally: the house, the food. Okay, he had the house in France, but if you spent two minutes actually talking to me, you'd know I would have loved Evan penniless. In fact, I nearly ended things because he was spending *too much* money on me.'

Erin's eyes widened, and Holly pounced.

'Oh, you didn't know that? No, well, perhaps if you spent some time actually learning about me as a person and what your brother's life in England was actually like, you would have already known that.'

Several people around the table were drawing sharp intakes of breath as if they were about to interrupt, but no one dared speak.

'You're right. I do get on well with Ben, as did Evan,' Holly continued. As she finally had Erin listening to her, it seemed like the right thing to keep going. 'They used to go cycling together a lot. Which again, you would have known, if you'd had any intention of speaking to him. But you didn't bother with that, did you? No, you were just too determined to get your attacks in. Would you rather Ben and I hated each other? That Hope got torn between the pair of us? Would that make you think better of me as a person? Of course it wouldn't, because you know nothing about me, and you have no desire to learn. You think your grief is the only one that's valid around this table, Erin, and it's not. Your parents have lost their only son. Their youngest child. Did you even think about that?'

'Holly. I'm—'

It was the first time Erin had tried to speak, but Holly wasn't going to let her. She had more to say, perhaps the most important piece so far, and she wasn't going to let anyone stop her.

'And as for Hope not being his, you really think that's what makes a family? And if you do, how insulting are you, not to me, but to your own family? To Catherine, and your dad.'

Anne had told Holly the story the very first time they'd spoken on a video call. She told Holly how she had got pregnant when she was young, to a complete loser, but thankfully, Jonathan had been there. He'd swept in and taken Catherine on as his own. The rest of the girls were his biologically, but Catherine was his only in name and heart.

'Your dad loves Catherine the same way he loves all of you. And for you to say that Evan wasn't capable of such a thing, particularly when he had the most phenomenal role model, well, it sounds to me like you didn't know your brother at all.'

It was only when Holly stopped that she felt the tears welling in her eyes. She had kept so many of her tears in since she'd arrived in America. Almost since she had first started telling people the news. She could feel the masks of smiles and positivity she had kept so firmly on her face slipping, as all the pain she had tried to supress rose within her. But she was damned if Erin was going to be the reason she finally released it.

With a deep inhalation, she blinked the tears away before standing up and looking at Anne.

'I'm ever so sorry,' she said, before shifting her gaze to Catherine and the other sisters. 'I didn't mean to make a scene. I'll leave the rest of you to enjoy your meal now.'

49

As Holly stood up and walked out of the dining room, no one objected. She half thought they might. That perhaps Erin would try to defend herself, or just bring Holly down further, but she didn't. She thought perhaps Catherine would follow, although what Holly expected her to say, she wasn't sure. As it was, no one followed and no one spoke.

Holly walked out into the hallway, her heart drumming against her chest. She shouldn't have made such a scene, she thought, but quickly changed her mind. She might not have known Evan as long as Erin, but she knew him well enough to know he would have been disgusted by the way his sister had spoken to her, and that was enough. Still, she couldn't remember the last time she had spoken to someone in such a manner and the after-effects of the adrenaline had left her pulse skipping.

Holly's intention was to head upstairs and give herself a couple of minutes to cool off further, but as she reached the hall, Jonathan came out of the playroom.

'Is everything all right, Holly?' he said. Hope was standing at his side, holding her grandad's hand as if it was the most natural thing in the world, though her face was slightly pale. 'We heard raised voices. Hope wanted to come and check you were okay.' He lowered his voice. 'Sorry, I tried to keep her with the others, but she wasn't having it. I didn't want her to get upset.'

'Thank you, Jonathan. It's fine, really it is,' Holly said. 'I'll take Hope now. Could you just tell the others I'm sorry for making a scene?'

Rather than responding immediately, Jonathan quirked his eyebrow and let out a sigh.

'Let me guess – Erin?'

Holly didn't respond, but she didn't need to.

Jonathan carried on. 'Honestly, it's like God thought I'd had it too easy with the other five, so he threw her into the mix, just to even it up a bit.' He let out a sad chuckle. 'I thought she'd grown out of it, but I guess this has thrown us all. Anne says it's the artistic side of her, but sometimes I think that's generous. She just has to make everything about her. Honestly, I can't apologise enough if she said anything that upset you. Which I'm sure she did.'

Holly nodded. She didn't want to get drawn into a conversation and had no intention of bad-mouthing Erin to Jonathan. It didn't matter how candidly he had just spoken to her; Erin was his daughter, and Holly knew he loved her with all his heart.

All Holly knew for certain was that coming here was a mistake. But there was no way she could back out of it now. Maybe, she thought, she would take a leaf out of Ben's book and spend the rest of her time at the mall.

'Thank you, Jonathan,' she said, before stretching her hand out to take Hope's. 'I think we're going to go upstairs and have a bath, aren't we?'

Hope looked at her mother and frowned.

'Hope had bath,' she said. 'Daddy gave Hope bath.'

'Is that right?' Holly replied. It would make sense. Ben probably gave her one while Holly was having a sleep, before he put her down for a nap. 'Does that mean you don't want another one?'

The thought percolated for only a couple of moments before a smile twisted on Hope's lips. But rather than replying, Hope tilted her head and looked up at her new grandad.

'I love baths,' she said.

50

Hope was still splashing around in the water when Ben came home. Holly heard the doorbell ring, which was followed a few moments later by footsteps on the staircase, after which came the knock on the bathroom door.

'It's open – you can come in,' Holly called.

'Hey, is everything okay?' Ben said walking through the door a moment later and gesturing to Hope. 'Did she get messy? I gave her a bath earlier.'

'I know. I just needed some air.'

'In the bathroom? With Hope?'

Holly let out a long sigh, before turning and looking at Ben. Her expression must have said it all.

'That bad?' he asked.

'That bad,' she replied.

With another groan, she turned back to Hope, who was currently playing with a water wheel. Anne had dug out a box of bath toys earlier in the day, and Hope was as happy as Larry. And not just in the bath, but here, in America. She'd already told Holly how much she loved the house and how much fun she'd been having with Grandad. She knew all of her cousins by name now, and although the pronunciation of Lauren sounded more like Lolly, it was clear the two got on fantastically. That was worth the trip, wasn't it? Holly tried to convince herself. If Holly hadn't brought her here, it would have been a relationship limited to video calls until they rang less and less and gradually stopped being part of each other's lives. There was no way Holly would let that happen now. Not having seen how much Hope loved her grandparents.

Still, she could have come later. After the funeral, perhaps. Jamie was only weeks away from having her baby, and Holly would never forgive herself if she wasn't in England when that happened. It terms of positives versus negatives on this trip, Holly knew which side was winning, but there was no way she was going to let Ben know that.

'We're going out tomorrow,' Holly said. 'Anne and Jonathan want to show me some places Evan liked growing up. It'll be good. I think it's just been too long cooped up, you know. You know, the plane, the house.'

It was as if her walk earlier in the day to the lake had been forgotten, although she couldn't deny a day without Erin's presence would definitely lift her mood a lot.

'I think I need some time with just Hope and me, too,' Holly added. 'But I'm not sure when that's going to happen.'

Ben looked as if he was about to reply, and probably offer a very logical solution Holly hadn't yet considered, when his phone started ringing. He pulled it out of his pocket, glanced at the screen, and frowned.

'Everything okay?'

'I think so,' he said. 'It's work. Sorry, I need to get this.'

'Sure, no problem,' Holly said, but before she had even

finished speaking, Ben had turned around and was walking out of the room.

Once again, Holly let out a deep sigh. How it was possible she felt tired again after all the hours she'd been sleeping, she had no idea, but as soon as Hope was out of the bath, she planned on curling up in bed with her.

She grabbed one of the toys and started pouring water over Hope's belly.

'Daddy gone. Daddy on phone?' Hope said, proving she had been fully aware of everything that had been going on, even though she'd been playing with her toys. She was going to be a masterful eavesdropper when she was older.

'It's the bank,' Holly replied. 'Your daddy works far too hard, but you're very lucky, aren't you? Having a daddy who's very clever like that.'

It was only Ben fielding work calls that made Holly think about the sweet shop. It had been an act of self-preservation, not thinking about it. She didn't have the mental capacity to worry about the business, what with everything else going on. In truth, she didn't have the mental capacity to deal with anything that was happening to her at the moment, but she trusted her dad and Caroline to be running the place just as well as she could. Although that thought caused another surge of guilt to rise in her.

Caroline had grief to deal with, too. Not at the same level as Holly, but Evan was her friend. And Holly knew Caroline. She would be doing everything she could to support Fin with the funeral arrangements and helping Jamie prepare for the imminent arrival of the baby, and all that, while trying to look after her own family, too, with young children who viewed Evan as an uncle to them. The sweet shop was an added pressure she almost certainly didn't need. And Holly's guilt wasn't confined to Caroline. Arthur was bound to be worried sick about Holly, both geographically and in her current mental state, and the last thing she wanted to do was put any pressure on him. Not with the way his heart was.

Deciding she needed to call them as soon as she could, Holly tried to hurry Hope along a little. After all, it wasn't like she actually needed a bath.

'Come on, you,' she said, reaching down to pick up her daughter. 'Let's get you out and get you dry.'

As was always the case, getting Hope out of the bath wasn't straightforward. She loved being in the water and would do anything for an extra five minutes, whether she was at the swimming pool, ankle-deep in the river in Bourton, or even, occasionally, standing out in the rain.

'Please, Mamma. Please! It's so big!' She slid to the side, out of Holly's reach, to prove her point. 'Hope stay in bath!'

Holly groaned. It really was a large bath, and as soon as Hope got out of it, Holly was going to start getting her ready for bed. Another part of their routine which was often far less simple than it sounded. Deciding that she could really do with relative quiet when she spoke to her family, Holly reconsidered her original idea and pulled her phone out of her pocket. There was no point waiting. She might as well speak to her parents now, although what she was going to tell them was another matter altogether.

51

Holly was an idiot. She realised it the moment the video call opened and her screen was in pitch darkness. Before she could say anything, a light flashed on, and her mother's face appeared, squinting into the camera.

'Holly? What is it, dear? What's wrong?'

Holly's guilt and feeling of stupidity intensified.

'I'm so sorry. I didn't think,' she said, glancing at her watch, not that it helped. It had automatically reset to the right time as soon as she landed, and she hadn't yet figured out how to work out the time difference. Not that she needed to know exactly what the time in the UK was. It was late. That much was obvious. 'Sorry, I'll go.'

'No, no, don't.' It was her father's voice who came through now. 'Don't be silly. We were hoping you'd ring.'

'I can ring you later,' Holly replied, although she didn't know when. 'What time is it now?' She tried to check, though her mother waved the comment away.

'Oh, don't worry about that,' she said. 'Tell us, how is everything there? Have you met Evan's sisters? I bet you have a lot to talk about.'

Both Holly's parents were sitting upright in the bed now, and her mother shifted the camera around so they both fitted onto the screen, although Holly wished she hadn't. It was even harder trying to be positive with both of them staring at her expectantly.

'Yes, yes, they were all here for dinner,' Holly said. For all she knew, they were still there now too, although only a couple of minutes ago, she had heard the door go and a car start in the driveway, so that might not be the case.

'And...' her mother pressed. 'How are they all holding up? How are *you* holding up?'

Now she was speaking to her parents, Holly wasn't sure what she actually wanted to say, or if she wanted to talk to them at all. She certainly didn't want to tell them everything that had happened with Erin, and she was sure they weren't expecting her to say that everything was all rosy. Yes, these people had lost a member of their family, but she didn't want to make her parents worry about her any more than they were already doing.

'It's really beautiful here,' Holly said, trying to focus on the positives. 'The scenery is incredible. I actually bumped into one of Evan's sisters down at the lake.' The memory of that moment, of running towards Parker screaming, flooded her mind, but Holly pushed it away. 'And we're going somewhere Evan loved tomorrow. And Hope is having a great time. She's being spoiled rotten, particularly by her grandad.'

'Her grandad, eh?' Holly's father said. 'He better not be taking my spot as the favourite. I'll be having words with him if that's the case.'

'Ignore him, love,' her mother said, slapping Arthur playfully on the arm as she spoke. 'I'm glad she's having fun. Where is our Hope?'

'She's right here,' Holly said, flipping the camera around so her parents could see Hope in the bath. For the next ten minutes, they chatted away, with Hope blowing bubbles off her hand, while Holly's mum and dad clapped and cheered obligingly. There was something incredibly soothing about the normality of it. Of her parents' voices and laughter. It was so easy and natural, Holly actually forgot that only an hour ago, she'd been downstairs, speaking to Evan's sister in a way she'd never spoken to anyone before in her life. It was a needed respite, and only when there were more bubbles on the bathroom floor than left in the tub did Holly flick the camera back around and refocus the conversation.

'How's everything at the shop going?' she asked. 'I messaged Caroline, and she said everything's fine, but I just wanted to check.'

'Everything's good,' her father said. 'Actually, I met Drey's girl-friend today.'

'Drey's girlfriend?'

'Lovely young lady, actually. Very nice.'

A flicker of warmth spread through Holly as she considered that maybe this relationship of Drey's was the real deal. Sure, she was young, but Agnes and Maud found love young too, and so had Caroline and Michael and you couldn't have dreamed of finding two more perfectly suited couples.

'I should let you go,' Holly said, suddenly aware of how long they had been talking. 'You probably have things you need to be getting on with.'

'Don't be silly,' her mother replied. 'We're your parents. That's what we're here for. To call, any time of day or night. Whenever you need us.'

'Thank you.'

'We mean it, Holly. Whenever you need us, we're there.'

It took several goodbyes from Hope before Holly finally hung up the phone and got her daughter out of the bath. Holly wrapped her in a towel that had been warming on the rail, before taking her through into the bedroom. For all the energy Hope had had in the bath, she was already yawning again. An act that Holly quickly mirrored. How Ben had kept going all day, she wasn't sure. Particularly as she didn't even see him sleep on the plane. Hopefully, he would be able to get a good night's sleep tonight, though.

She was thinking how she should tell Ben she was fine with Hope for the rest of the evening and he should head down and call it a night, when there was a knock on the door.

Holly's stomach churned as she envisioned Anne or one of Evan's sisters standing outside the room, wanting to talk to her. As selfish as she felt, she had only just fully calmed down and stopped being furious – at both herself and at Erin. Even if it was Catherine or Ashley, she didn't know if she had the strength to speak to them. But she could hardly refuse. They would know she wasn't asleep. Not with the light on.

With a deep breath, she called, 'Yes, come in.'

The door creaked open, but rather than one of Evan's sisters or any member of his family standing there, it was Ben. His phone was still hanging in his hand, and for the first time, Holly saw exactly how exhausted he looked. He hadn't looked that bad in the bathroom a little while ago, had he? Surely she would have noticed.

'I was just about to come and find you,' she said. 'I thought you might want to get an early night.'

Rather than refusing or accepting the offer, which Holly had thought were the only two options, Ben scoffed instead.

'Wouldn't that be great?' he said. 'I'm sorry, Holly. We need to talk.'

52

They may not have been a couple for very long, but given that Ben and Holly had Hope together and had been through so much, Holly knew she could probably read him better than any of her other friends. And right now, she knew that whatever he wanted to tell her wasn't good. With a new sense of nervousness buzzing in her veins, she finished tugging Hope's top down and looked at Ben.

'What is it? What's wrong?'

Ben looked between Holly and Hope before coming into the bedroom. After lifting up Hope, Holly moved over on the bed, making sure that there was room for him to take a seat, but he remained standing.

'That was work on the phone just then,' he said. 'I've got to go back.'

'Back?'

'Back to England,' Ben clarified. 'Something happened with a merger we'd got planned. I don't want to go into it right now, but it's a lot of stress and it's pretty much all on my head. I wouldn't have come if I thought for one second that this could happen. I'm so sorry.'

Ben hadn't needed to clarify about him being stressed. It was all too clear from his expression that whatever was going on had put him under a significant amount of pressure.

'Work's already been online and booked me a flight out of Seattle. It leaves just before midnight.'

'Tonight?' Holly said, before glancing down at her phone. 'That's in less than four hours.'

'I know. I've spoken to them. They know it's a family bereavement. And they're happy to pay for Hope as well, you know, because I'd taken the time off specifically. I don't want to leave you here, but I'm sure you can change your flights to come with me. Or...'

'Or?' Holly said, feeling there was something more he wanted to add.

'Or I could take Hope with me by myself. I'm sure your mum wouldn't mind a couple of extra days with her while I'm working. Or Jamie, for that matter. You know, if you want a bit more time with Evan's family. But honestly...'

Ben paused and his bottom lip disappeared beneath his top teeth.

'But honestly, what?' Holly said, confused at how he was planning on ending his sentence.

As it was, he took a deep breath in before he tried.

'I heard what happened at dinner with Erin. Anne told me when I came in. She wanted me to check you were all right.'

Holly didn't know why this felt like a betrayal of trust on Anne's part. She had obviously only told Ben about the incident because she was worried Holly was still upset. It also made sense why none of them had come and checked on her, too.

'Maybe they needed more time before you came here,' Ben

continued. 'Things are so incredibly raw for them, and for you, too. Ridiculously raw. You've not even had a chance to start grieving yet.'

'Everybody grieves differently,' Holly snapped back. She didn't know why this comment about not grieving got to her so much. Perhaps because it was absurd. How on earth could she not be grieving? She had lost Evan.

'You're right,' Ben said, his tone soft. 'But maybe it would be a good idea to come back home with me tonight. Then, in a year, or maybe even just six months, you could come back here again. If you're feeling up to it.'

Holly understood what Ben was saying. There was no doubt a couple of her actions had been a little out of character, but that had hardly been all her fault. And she had considered more than once that coming hadn't been the right thing to do. But how could she leave now? Hope had barely spent one day with her grandfather, who adored her. The last thing she wanted to do was tear her away from here and her grandparents. Not when she'd already lost Evan. Though Hope was only half Holly's reason for not wanting to head back to the Cotswolds.

'I can't go. Not yet,' she said. 'I'm not ready, Ben. If I go back, I'll have to help Fin with all the arrangements. I'll have to go back to the empty house. And I just need a bit more time, you know.' Holly also wanted to say how there was still so much more she wanted to see and do while on this side of the Atlantic, but she suspected Ben would consider that part of the *not grieving* she was supposedly doing.

As she waited for him to respond, Ben's lips pressed together so tightly, they formed a thin line, and Holly knew there was more he wanted to say.

'I don't feel great leaving you here on your own like this,' he said.

'It will be fine. Anne and Jonathan will look after me. And most of Ben's sisters are wonderful. Honestly, I will be fine.' Holly stood up, stepped forward, and took Ben by the hand. 'I really appreciate you doing this. I do. And you've already done so much for me. But I'm going to have to stand on my own two feet, sooner or later. And I think I should learn to do it here. Okay?'

Ben nodded. Holly knew he wasn't convinced, but he didn't say any more. Instead, he looked at Hope.

'And I don't suppose there's any point in me asking again if you want me to take her back to England with me?'

'Not a chance,' Holly said, before glancing down at her daughter. 'Hope, honey, come and give your daddy a big hug goodbye. He's going to have to leave and go on a plane a bit sooner than planned.'

'You're leaving?' Hope said, a sudden look of fear on her face. 'Forever? Like Evvy?'

Less than a second later, Hope was sobbing her heart out.

53

'Hope, darling, you need to calm down. Please. It's okay. You'll see Daddy again. I promise you'll see Daddy again. Soon. He's just going to England a little bit before us. That's all.'

Holly doubted Hope could even hear what was being said over her wails, but she kept trying, holding her daughter tight against her as she rocked back and forth, offering all the comforting words and sounds she could, even though she wasn't 100 per cent sure they were true. How could she ever be 100 per cent sure about such a thing again? Had Hope started wailing when Evan handed her back to Wendy, outside the sweet shop only a week ago, Holly would have assured her it would all be all right. She would have said that she would see Evvy soon too. And she would have been wrong.

'Come here, Hopey,' Ben said, stretching out his arms for her and forcing Holly back out of her memories. Holly didn't want to let her daughter go, even though she knew Ben was just as capable of comforting Hope as she was. She wanted to hold on to her and never let her go, but Ben was leaving, and if it was the other way around, he would never have dreamed of preventing Holly from a proper farewell.

It took them over fifteen minutes to convince Hope it would only be a short-term separation, and they would see Ben again the moment they got home.

'And Evvy?' Hope asked, having pieced together this new information with perfect two-year-old logic. 'We see Evvy too?'

'No, not Evvy, Hope,' Ben said, as Holly's mouth turned dry. 'Remember, Evvy is with his granny and grandad and it's too far for us to go there and visit.'

'We go on plane?' Hope suggested. It was enough to make Holy's heart throb.

'There are no planes that go there,' Holly said, knowing that she had to say something.

'You will see me soon, though. Because lots and lots of planes go to England,' Ben said, redirecting the conversation flawlessly. Probably, Holly suspected, for her sake as much as Hope's. 'I will speak to you as soon as I land. I promise. But you have to be extra good, okay? I want you to take care of your mummy on the plane when you come back. You're going to have to be even more grown-up. Can you do that for me?'

Hope nodded. Her eyes were still red-rimmed, but she had at least stopped her tears. 'I can do that.'

'Okay. Thank you, darling.'

Ben looked at Holly, and she could see the concern heavy in his eyes.

'I guess I better get packing,' he said.

54

Ben left just an hour later. At which point, Hope once again descended into tears.

'Why don't you let me look after her, sweetie?' Anne said. 'You can have a bit of quiet time...'

There was something about the way Anne finished her sentence that made it sound like a pause. Like there was something she wanted to say, but she wasn't sure how to. Not for the first time that evening, Holly wished people could just finish their sentences, rather than causing her pulse to rocket as she waited in fear of whatever was coming next.

'Is there something else you wanted me to do?' Holly said. 'Did you want Hope and me to move into the office?'

'What? No. Not at all. Unless you want to?'

Holly considered the offer for a moment. Would she prefer to be in a room that hadn't been Evan's? She wasn't sure, but what she did know was that she had no desire to move all her belonging downstairs, even if she knew the others would help.

'I think I'd prefer to stay where I am. If that's okay?'

'Of course,' Anne replied. 'I was going to say that Erin and

Emily have gone out and Ashley's gone with them. I think she's hoping to talk some sense into her sister.'

So that was it, Holly realised. Anne wanted to bring up Erin, and probably the scene Holly had made at dinner, too.

'Mel and Catherine are still downstairs with Tommy,' Anne continued. 'They're all staying tonight. And the children, obviously. Ashley'll probably come back too. I didn't know if you wanted to go have a drink with them. You know, without us oldies hanging about. There's a nice little bar a mile or so down the road. Jonathan can always drop you off and pick you all up?'

It was such a sweet offer. A maternal offer. To have Holly's not-quite-father-in-law drop her and the others off at the pub and pick them back up like they were a bunch of youths who had just reached the legal drinking age. She suspected it was something he did fairly often when they had the children stay. Not that any of them were children.

'That's really lovely, but I don't think I've got it in me to head out tonight,' Holly said honestly.

'Of course. Of course. Well, there's plenty of wine in the fridge. Or beer if that's what you drink? We've probably got some spirits, too. You know you can help yourself to anything.'

'Thank you,' Holly said. It was clear Anne was desperate to make her feel as welcome as possible, but it wasn't just that Holly didn't have it in her to head out. She didn't have the strength to socialise any more either.

'I think it's probably best if I just head to bed with Hope,' she said. 'I don't know why I'm so tired; I slept for hours today already.'

'Grief does things to the body, dear. Different things to all of us. You take all the time you want. I was thinking we'd go for a walk to Evan's Creek tomorrow if you're up for it, but if you're not, it's really not a problem.'

'Evan's Creek?' Holly said.

'It's the place we named him after. Would you believe it?'

Holly did, absolutely, and she knew there was no way she could miss an opportunity to see somewhere that was as important to Evan's heritage and who he was.

'Thank you, Anne. Thank you for everything,' she said.

With Hope still in her arms, Holly hugged her not-quite-mother-in-law, then headed upstairs.

The plan was to have a great night's sleep and be ready and alert for the walk the next day, but as Holly was learning, things never went to plan.

55

Hope had to be sleepy. She was sleepy. She kept yawning, and her eyes kept closing for longer and longer, but each time she started to drift off, she would jerk back awake and start talking away, or wanting to play with Holly and her toys. Or have Holly read her yet another story, even though she'd read through the small selection of books they'd brought half a dozen times already. There were limits to such things. Even with Julia Donaldson books.

'Come on, Hopey. Mummy needs you to sleep. Please try.'

More than once, Holly considered going downstairs and having a drink with the others, but by the time she had made the decision, she heard them wishing one another a good night and the landing light went off.

At three-thirty in the morning, Hope finally gave up the ghost and fell into a deep sleep. And Holly was sure she would follow suit straight away. Only she didn't.

Even with Hope having drifted off, Holly found it impossible to find a comfortable position to sleep in. The bed was the perfect firmness, yet she tossed and turned, and soon the bed wasn't the only thing keeping her awake. Her stomach growled loudly and once it started, it had no intention of stopping.

When had she last eaten? She had picked at dinner, not quite the same way as Erin had, but probably not much more. None of them had eaten that much, and Holly suspected at least three-quarters of the leftovers remained downstairs in the fridge.

As if confirming this, her stomach growled again. There was bound to be something down there she could take. Something little, just to fill her up enough that she could fall asleep.

With one last check on Hope, Holly got out of bed and headed downstairs.

Walking as quietly as she could, she was heading to the kitchen when she saw the light on in the dining room. With a change of direction, she stepped forward and peered through the door. Anne was sitting at the table, wiping tears as they streamed down her cheeks, while she stared at something in front of her. In that moment, a single memory flooded through Holly: the first proper conversation she and Evan had had. It was on the plane to Jamie's hen party – she'd been less than impressed with his self-assured ways and had even tried to trade seats so she didn't have to sit next to him.

Her pulse pounded at the memory. Thinking back on that made her heart and head ache. What if they'd agreed, and she hadn't sat next to Evan on the flight?

Another memory flitted into her mind: a moment from later that holiday. What if she hadn't gone downstairs that night and found him poring over his laptop?

What if she hadn't wanted to go for brunch when they'd been in the Lake District? Or what if she'd kissed him, just for a minute longer, so by the time they reached the lake, there was nothing Evan could have done? She knew it was wrong to wish for such a thing, but there were so many 'what ifs', it made her muscles weak and a small gasp escaped from her lips.

'Holly?' Anne's head came up from the table. 'I'm sorry, love, I didn't see you there. You can't sleep either?'

Holly shook her head. 'I was just going to get something to eat, actually. Don't let me disturb you.'

'No, no, don't be silly,' Anne replied. 'You're not disturbing me. Come on in. I was just looking at some photos. Do you want to see?'

Holly didn't want to interrupt Anne's time, but she could tell that she wanted Holly to join her.

Upon stepping into the dining room, Holly could finally see what Anne had been staring at: a large photo album bursting at the seams.

'We had to get them all their own birthday cakes,' Anne said as Holly looked down at the open page. The children didn't look much older than Hope. Had she not known who she was looking at, she definitely wouldn't have recognised Erin and Emily. But there was something about the smile, Evan's smile, that was 100 per cent him. Even at that age.

'Their first birthday's the only one they shared a cake for,' Anne continued. 'And honestly, well, we tried on their second birthday, too. My goodness, what a mess. Each wanted to be the first one and the last one to blow out the candles. They couldn't just do it together. No. Then there'd been an argument over who got to eat the first slice of cake. Honestly, the whole thing nearly drove me insane, so after that, we just went for one each. Three cakes every year. And I can't bake for toffee. No, I cannot. It was their aunt who had to make them. You'd think she'd do it for free, you know, being her nephew and nieces and everything, but of course, that wasn't the case.'

A smile creased Anne's face, but it didn't last for long. In an instant, her eyes were back down at the photo album, once again welling. It felt like only a minute ago Holly had been comforting Hope and that had been hard enough to do. Holly didn't know if she had it in her to comfort Anne. She knew she should try, though, given everything Anne had done for her.

Holly glanced down at the album when a thought flickered in her mind. The same one that she'd had only a few minutes ago, standing outside the door. And so, she reached her hand out and placed it on top of Anne's.

'Do you know the first time Evan and I had a proper conversation was like this, in the middle of the night, when the rest of the house was dead to the world, but we were wide awake and couldn't sleep?'

Anne sniffed as she looked up at Holly. The smile on her lips was tight and forced, but the words that followed were spoken with genuine love.

'Can you tell me about it?'

56

They moved to the kitchen, taking the photo album with them, although Anne didn't open it again while Holly was with her. Instead, she listened to Holly's stories, from the very first meeting at the airport, to the Vespa and the bunny rabbits. Even though Holly knew Anne would have already heard some of the tales, either from Evan, or Holly herself on a video call, she didn't filter them. She told her everything she could.

She told Anne about the giant frying pan Evan had bought for doing pancakes, even though it was far too big to fit in any of the cupboards in the kitchen, and she told her how he had put an offer in on a house for them without telling her, but then withdrew it again, because he didn't want Holly to think he was trying to control things or take it all too fast. But Holly had never felt like that with Evan. Sure, she had hated the way he overspent on her, but that was because she didn't need things. She didn't need to be spoiled. Not when she was with Evan. He was all she ever needed.

It was with a heavy heart that Holly told Anne how, after that first week, she and Evan had felt like an inevitability. Of course, there was that slight mishap at the very beginning of the relationship. There didn't feel anything inevitable about travelling in a taxi through the south of France in search of a heliport. But after that, everything had felt like it would just fall into place. Just like finding the perfect house had. There was no need to rush marriage, or children. It would all come. At least that was what Holly had thought.

'You know, he felt the same,' Anne said. She had made them both herbal teas and put out various nibbly foods for them to pick at. It might have been Holly's imagination, or just the change of lighting, but she couldn't help but feel that a bit more colour had returned to Anne's cheeks. 'He told us he'd met the girl he was going to marry after that trip to France. He was smitten, hook, line, and sinker. And I knew you had to be someone special, because Evan wouldn't have felt that way for anyone who wasn't truly remarkable.'

Holly picked up her fruit tea and held it to her lips. She wasn't thirsty. She just didn't know how to reply. She didn't think she was remarkable. Not for one second. Not the way Evan was. He had achieved so much in his life. He had seen so much and been to so many places. Not that Holly didn't feel proud of what she'd accomplished with the sweet shop, but it was a very different kettle of fish, running a tiny sweet shop in the Cotswolds, to the type of businesses Evan ran.

'I don't know what he saw in me,' Holly said truthfully. 'I know we made each other laugh, though. And I always felt safe with him. Like I could tell him anything in the world, and he'd never judge me. That's how it's meant to be, isn't it? When you love someone.'

'It is.'

'And now he's gone.'

It didn't matter how many times she said it, it still didn't feel real. It was like she was talking about someone else's life, and not hers.

Anne reached her hand across the table, most likely to take Holly's the way Holly had done to her previously, and yet before they touched, a loud bang rang out from the front door.

'What on earth?' Anne said, jumping to her feet. Holly did the same. Her eyes darted to the clock on the wall, which told her it was 5 a.m. For a split second, she thought it was a burglar, trying to break in through the glass of the door, but then a moment later, there was the sound of a key in the lock.

The door opened, and Erin tumbled through. She could barely stand up straight, and had left the door wide open, although Ashley promptly followed inside and was standing much more upright as she turned around and gently pushed the door closed.

'Come on, we need to get you to bed,' Ashley whispered, trying to help her sister up, but Erin shook her away. Her arms flailed as she stumbled out of Ashley's reach, but as she moved, Erin's gaze fell into the kitchen. For the first time, her posture shifted into fully upright.

With a snarl on her face, she took a step towards the room and looked straight at Holly.

'Why the hell is she still here?' she spat.

57

Erin was drunk and well past the normal level of social acceptability. Swaying on the spot, she slurred her words.

'She shouldn't be here,' she said. No one was in any doubt as to who she was talking about. 'I don't like her here.'

'What are you doing?' Anne hissed. 'You'll wake all the children. Hope only got to sleep a couple of hours ago.'

Erin snorted and shrugged.

'And? She's a kid. She can sleep whenever she wants. They can all sleep whenever they want.'

'Come on, Erin,' Ashley said, trying for a second time to get a hold of her sister, but yet again, Erin shook her away.

'Get off me! What are you doing? We're having a conversation. I'm talking to Mum. I'm talking to *her*.' The last word she spat from her lips with so much force, Holly flinched. Holly hadn't thought it would be possible for someone to say a single syllable with such venom, and yet Erin was making it look like the easiest thing in the world.

'No, you're being abusive. That's what you're doing,' Ashley corrected. 'You need to go upstairs and go to bed.'

Holly stood there, not sure what she was supposed to do. She didn't want to be there. She knew that much. The conversation at dinner had been the last time she'd seen Erin, and from what Anne had said about her staying at Emily's for the night, Holly hadn't expected to see her again anytime soon. If at all. Part of Holly had thought, or maybe even hoped, that now Erin had seen Holly and Hope and said her piece, she wouldn't come back to her parents' house until after they'd left. Clearly, that wasn't the case.

For the first time since Erin and Ashley had returned home, Anne left Holly's side. She strode towards her youngest daughter with a face like thunder.

'This is not acceptable, Erin,' she said. 'I don't know where you've been, but you absolutely stink. You need to go upstairs. Sleep this off. You can have a shower in the morning.'

Erin scowled, but remained silent. Possibly because she was now having to hold on to the wall to keep her balance.

Holly knew from her own experience that there was something unique about mother-daughter relationships. Holly adored her mother with her whole heart, but they still butted heads. Wendy would forever be Holly's mother and, as such, would always believe she knew what was best in a situation, regardless of whether that was true. Take the incident with Giles buying Holly a house to live in. Her mother had held on to that secret for months and months because she believed it was for the best and if Holly had not found out by herself, she might have held on to it indefinitely. It had taken a long time to build back those bridges of trust.

That had been a very different situation, of course, but it was clear from the way Erin's face was scrunched into a snarl that this was one of those occasions when she didn't want her mother's advice.

'I'm a grown woman,' she slurred out eventually. 'If I want a drink of wine, I'll have one.'

'A drink?' Anne said. 'Looks like you've drunk an entire vineyard dry from where I'm standing. And you might be a grown woman, but if you come into my home like this again, cursing and crashing around while my grandchildren are asleep, you will find yourself very unwelcome.'

'Don't worry, I don't plan on hanging around here. Why would I want to do that when you welcome Judases into Evan's bedroom?'

At that, she turned around and staggered up the stairs. As Ashley moved to follow her, Anne spoke again.

'I thought you were meant to be keeping an eye on her. Making sure she didn't get too out of hand?'

Ashley let out a brief sigh and rolled her eyes. 'Really, Mum? You think I didn't try?'

With that, Ashley followed Erin up the stairs, softly calling her sister's name.

Only after hearing the click of the bathroom door did Anne release an audible breath. 'I'm so sorry,' she started, but Holly wouldn't hear it. Of all the people who didn't need to apologise to her, Anne was at the top of the list.

'Come on,' Holly said, looping her arms into the older woman's. 'Why don't we finish our drinks and give them time to get settled upstairs, then we should go to bed too. I think we both need some rest.'

Anne nodded before looking Holly straight in the eyes. A sad smile hovered on her lips. 'It's easy to see why he loved you so much,' she said.

58

Holly felt like she had barely closed her eyes when morning rolled around and she was expected to get up again.

'Five minutes, Hopey,' Holly said, groggily as Hope tried tugging the covers off her. 'Mum just needs five more minutes' sleep, then we'll get up.'

'Hope awake!' Hope said, her loud and cheerful voice a sign that she had got a far better sleep than Holly.

'Yes, Hope awake, but Mummy asleep,' Holly tried again. 'Just read your books for a minute, baby girl, okay? There's a good girl.'

Reading books in bed when she woke up was part of Hope's normal routine, and Holly knew she was guaranteed an extra ten or fifteen minutes before she tried to get her up again. In the end, though, it wasn't Hope who woke Holly, but a knock on the door.

At first, Holly thought it was part of her dream. One knock and then another, getting gradually louder and louder. It wasn't until Catherine's voice accompanied the sounds that Holly finally opened her eyes.

'Hey,' Catherine said, poking her head around the door. 'I didn't want to disturb you, but Mel and I are taking the kids to the park. We thought you might want us to take Hope too. Give you a bit more time to sleep?'

Holly's mind processed the question as quickly as it could in her drowsy state. More sleep was definitely what Holly wanted, but she didn't want Evan's sisters to have to worry about looking after Hope. That was her job.

'Thank you. Maybe we'll head down a little later and join you,' she said, through several wide yawns.

Unfortunately, she wasn't the only one to have an opinion on the matter.

'Hope park!' Hope shouted excitedly. 'Hope go park!'

'Later, darling,' Holly said, still struggling to keep her eyes open. 'In a little bit.'

'We don't mind,' Catherine said. 'Like I said, we wanted to give you some more time. And Lauren has been asking about seeing Hope again from the moment she woke up.'

'Hope see Lolly. Hope go park?'

Holly could remember the days where she could have a conversation in front of her daughter, and Hope would have no idea what had been said. Those days were very much behind them.

'I haven't given her breakfast, or changed her nappy, or anything yet,' Holly started, but Catherine was already walking into the room with her arms open wide.

'Come on, Hopey,' she said. 'Let's you and I go have some fun and let your mummy get a bit more sleep. How does that sound?'

Holly wanted to thank Catherine. She wanted to say she appreciated her so much, not just for this, but for yesterday, too. But she didn't say a thing. Because before Catherine had even closed the door, Holly was sound asleep again.

59

When Holly finally woke up, she actually felt refreshed and, given how the last week had gone, that was something she hadn't expected. She stretched out, easing the clicks and cricks in her legs and neck, before rolling out of bed and heading over to the window, where she was about to pull open the curtains, when she heard a loud screech, the tone of which she immediately recognised.

Slipping on her slippers, Holly headed downstairs in search of Hope. It wasn't hard to find her. All she had to do was follow the squeals of laughter.

'Mamma!' Hope called as Holly stepped into the playroom. The room was darker than Holly expected, and all the curtains drawn, which seemed strange for so early in the day, but she paid it little mind.

All the children were there, along with Evan's parents, Mel and Ashley. Hope was currently dressed in full pirate regalia, complete with eye-patch, trousers that were at least six inches too long for her, and a sword. Unlike most costumes sold in shops nowadays, this one wasn't made from cheap flammable plastic. The eye-patch was leather and appeared to be hand-stitched, while the sword had a wooden handle.

'Mamma, Hope a pirate!' Hope said, although the word came out more like pie-et. 'Look, sword! Swoosh, swoosh?'

She swung the sword from side to side, narrowly missing Lauren, who was next to her dressed in a turquoise princess get-up. Just like the pirate outfit, the dress was a beautiful quality, with beadwork around the neckline and a lace trim.

'Careful, Hopey,' Holly said, reaching her hand out and taking hold of the sword to stop it from hitting anyone.

'Sorry,' Mel said. 'I thought it would be fun to get the dressing-up box out. Lauren always loves it. And she has good taste too. That dress was my favourite growing up. Hope went straight for the pirate, though. I wondered if Evan told her about it.'

'This was Evan's?' Holly said, looking at the outfit in wonder. Sure, it looked a little worn in places, but she'd thought the patches were part of the costume. It certainly didn't look thirty years old.

'Mum's a secret hoarder,' Mel said, at which Ashley and Jonathan chuckled, although Anne offered more of a mock pout.

'It's not hoarding, it's looking after things properly and not letting go of them just because they go out of fashion. You lot had years of fun with these, and with six of you, I knew I was going to get at least one grandchild who would make the most of them too.'

Now that Hope had shown Holly her costume, she was back to playing with her cousins, laughing away as they dug in the box and pulled out various other items, including a tiara, which Hope promptly placed on her head, though the eye-patch remained.

'So, I'm guessing you feel better after that sleep?' Jonathan said. 'I heard you had quite a late one last night. No doubt you needed all that rest.'

It was then that Holly realised she had no idea how long she'd slept. Or how long the others had been looking after Hope. Obviously long enough to go to the park and come back. Hopefully, she could repay Mel and Catherine by watching their children at some point in the week.

'What time is it?' she said, to no one in particular.

Rather than replying, the adults in the room exchanged a look. That wasn't the type of thing people normally did when someone asked what the time was, was it?

'You obviously needed a good recharge,' Anne said after a pause. 'I'm sure all that sleep did you good.'

Holly frowned. 'What time is it?' she said again. 'How long was I asleep?'

She looked directly at Ashley as she spoke this time. If anyone was going to give her a straight answer, she was sure it would be her, but even Ashley looked a little pained as she spoke.

'It's half past five?' she said, almost as if it were a question.

'Half past five?' Holly said, sure she must have misheard her. 'Half past five in the evening?'

'Well, late afternoon.' Mel tried to help. Holly felt her stomach drop out from within her. She only had six days in America to learn about Evan. The first one had been close to a disaster, and now she had slept entirely through the second one. She had lost an entire day.

60

It was too late and too dark to go for a walk, and while Anne offered various other suggestions, like going to the mall, or out for dinner, Hope had – according to Mel – been up since around ten, and Holly knew that if there was any chance of getting her back into some sort of routine, she would need to go to bed at a normal time. And so they decided to stay in, though Holly's first task was to ring Ben.

She had several missed calls from him as, true to his word, the moment he landed, he'd tried to get through. Given how Ben had a much better idea of different time zones, Holly pretended her phone had run out of battery and that was why she was so late speaking to him. The last thing she wanted was for him to think she couldn't look after Hope without him there. When she told him about the battery and not being able to find her charger, she wasn't sure he believed her, but he smiled anyway.

'So today went well?' he checked. 'How was everything with you know who?'

The fact that even Ben wouldn't say Erin's name couldn't be a good thing.

'I've not seen her today,' Holly said truthfully. 'She left before I got up. She's spending some time at Emily's.'

'And that's good?'

'I guess so.'

A slight pause filtered down the line before Ben spoke again. 'Jamie sends her love. She seems to have got even bigger in the forty-eight hours since I left. I'm not sure that should be possible.'

Holly chuckled, although her laughter was brief. Her mind shifted logically from Jamie to Fin, but she didn't want it to. She didn't want to think about Fin and everything he had to do. She hated how selfish that made her, but it was hardly the only thing she hated about herself at the moment.

'I better go, Ben,' Holly said, as she waved Hope over to say goodbye to her father. 'We're having a night watching Evan's old school plays.'

'Really?' Ben said. 'Is that a good idea?'

Even with Ben on the other side of the Atlantic, Holly still found it difficult to deal with his negative attitude towards her grieving process.

'Yes, it is,' she replied. 'According to the family, it'll make me laugh. A lot.'

Ben's lips twisted slightly, but he didn't say any more until Hope appeared on the screen.

'I'll speak to you tomorrow, okay, Hopey? Love you, baby.'

'Love you, Daddy. See soon,' Hope replied, before Holly hung up the phone. For some reason, hearing her say those words felt unusually hard. Not the 'love you' part. Holly loved hearing Hope say that. But the 'see you soon' bit. She said the same thing to Evan each time they spoke on the phone, and one day, it just stopped being true.

Refusing to be drawn back into the melancholy, Holly reached down and picked Hope up.

'Come on,' she said. 'Let's go see what these videos are like, shall we?'

61

It didn't take long for Holly to realise why the family had thought she would find it amusing to see Evan's early school plays. They were hysterical. Or at least, he was.

'Honestly, I don't even know why they allowed him on the stage half the time,' Jonathan said, as he topped up Holly's wine-glass. 'Of course, they couldn't give him a lead role because he couldn't sing for toffee. And he wouldn't have bothered to learn the lines either.'

'Really?' Holly said. The Evan she had known was so hard-working, it was impossible to imagine him any other way. But apparently, he hadn't always been like that.

'Oh, he was lazy when he was little. Too smart for his own good, that was his problem.' Anne took over the conversation. 'Got stuff so quick, he didn't have to bother half the time, and if he didn't get something straight away, and he had to work at it, then he didn't want to know. It's a shame, because he would have made a wonderful Oliver.'

'If Oliver hadn't had to sing,' Ashley joined in.

Anne scowled.

Rather than being given any lead roles, Evan was cast as such characters as Munchkin Number Seven, Lost Boy Number Eleven, and Holly's personal favourite, The Confused Card in *Alice in Wonderland*. Although according to his parents, he hadn't meant to look so confused; it was just that at the start of the play, when he looked down at his costume, and saw the numbers looking up at him, he assumed he was holding it the wrong way and switched it back around.

'That's what he said at least,' Jonathan said. 'Not that we bought it. The moment he got a laugh, he knew he was onto a good thing and carried on. For someone who always claimed to hate the stage, he really could entertain.'

Holly watched the flickering image on the screen. Every now and again, the camera would shift off the stage and look down the row at Anne, and Catherine and the other girls, who had all come to watch the triplets perform. Holly's heart was swelling and tightening simultaneously. In a few years' time, Hope would be up on a stage like that, and when Holly turned the camera away from the action, who would be there, next to her? Or rather, who wouldn't? Of course, she wouldn't have to attend any of Hope's plays alone. There would be Ben and Georgia, not to mention her parents. But Evan wouldn't be there. She would be the mum with nobody's hand to hold.

Again, Holly shook the thought away and tried to enjoy the moment, fixing her attention on the young, familiar-looking girl who was now on the middle of the stage.

Unlike Evan, Emily had a beautiful voice and had at least a small solo in most of the performances they watched. But one triplet was notably absent.

Half of Holly wanted to say nothing. To just be grateful that Erin wasn't with them now either, but eventually curiosity got the better of her. Especially considering the way she had imagined them doing everything together.

'How come Erin isn't in these?' she asked.

'Oh, Erin refused. Said she wanted to do the set instead. And so that's what she did. Every play.'

Holly felt her forehead crease in confusion. 'But aren't they, like, eight? Didn't they get made to be in it?'

'You've met Erin,' Jonathan said. 'Do you really think you could make her do anything?'

Holly turned her eyes back to the screen. The sets were all beautiful, but she doubted that had much to do with an eight-year-old. Still, Erin must have been talented for her teachers to let her help in such a manner. Whenever Evan had mentioned Erin, he had always talked about her art, and Holly had previously imagined that when she and Evan first visited his family, Erin would take them down to the studio and show them some of her work. Perhaps, Holly had daydreamed, they might even have bought a piece to hang in their house. She couldn't imagine that happening now.

Holly could feel herself being drawn back into her thoughts when Hope let out a long yawn. For the last ten minutes, Hope had been lying with her head on Holly's lap, and her eyes had just begun to sag as the last recording came to a stop. It was only just gone nine, meaning that Holly hadn't even been up for four hours, but given how much she wanted to make the most of the next day, she lifted Hope into her arms and stood up.

'Please don't think me rude, but I thought I might put Hope to bed, and have a long read in the bath, if that's okay with you?' she said. 'Then hopefully I'll be a bit more active tomorrow.'

'Of course it isn't rude,' Anne said, standing up and hugging her. 'Like I said when you arrived, if you need to sleep all day, then that's what you should do.'

Like most things Anne said, it was very sweet, but Holly hadn't travelled all this way to sleep when she had a perfectly good bed at home. She smiled the best she could as she shifted Hope around on her shoulder.

'Thank you, but the last thing I want is to lose another day,' she said. 'Tomorrow, we are definitely going to Evan's Creek.'

62

Just like Hope the night before, Holly quickly fell in love with the oversized bathtub. While she couldn't concentrate on her book quite the way she'd hoped, her body softened into the hot running water and bubbles. Holly had always loved hot baths, not warm ones. Hot, where the steam was rolling from the top of the water, and she continued to top it up every time it cooled even marginally. Her aim that night had been to soak away in the water for as long as possible – something she didn't normally have a problem with – but she had barely closed her eyes when a memory hit.

'Perhaps if I'm still in the bath when you get back, you can join me?'

That was what she'd said to Evan when he'd headed out to grab them some wine and food at the cottage. That was the moment he disappeared with his bag, and Holly first seriously considered how he could be planning on proposing that weekend.

The thought seized around her ribs, stifling her breath. The previously perfect bath suddenly felt scalding hot. She leapt from the tub, splashing water over the floor before grabbing a towel. With water still dripping from her hair, she slumped to the ground and held her hand to her mouth, refusing to let the tears fall.

So not only had she lost Evan now, but she had lost the life-long love of a good bath.

* * *

Holly didn't have the best sleep ever, but she didn't really expect to. It was gone midnight before she finally drifted off, and even then, she woke up every hour until five, at which point, it was only two hours before the alarm.

In a very unusual turn of events, even as the alarm jerked Holly back into the world, Hope remained fast asleep.

'This jet lag is really doing a number on you, isn't it?' Holly said, gently stroking her daughter's arm until her eyelids began to flutter. 'Come on, baby girl, we need to both get up, otherwise it's going to be impossible to sleep later.'

She scooped Hope up in her arms and pulled her in for a cuddle. Gradually, the shroud of sleep lifted, and Hope sat upright before grabbing her favourite bunny to hold.

'Hope hungry,' she said.

No 'Good morning' or, 'Love you, Mummy' to start the day with the way Hope normally did. Just, 'Hope hungry.'

Holly thought about the comment for a moment before she replied.

'Yeah, me too. Let's go get some food.'

Downstairs, Anne was already in the kitchen, dressed and with a full face of makeup on. A wide smile lit up her eyes as she saw Holly and Hope.

'I didn't know if we were going to see you this morning,' she said, before holding out her hand to Hope. 'How are you, sweetie? Did you sleep well?'

'Hope hungry,' Hope said again.

A glimmer of relief sparked in Holly. At least it hadn't been personal.

'Well, what do you know? I was about to make breakfast!' Anne said. 'What do you think about some pancakes? Blueberry or chocolate chip?'

'Boobie pancakes,' Hope said. 'Evvy make boobie pancakes.'

'Does he?' Anne looked at Holly and raised her eyebrow, at which point, Holly felt a slight tinge of embarrassment colour her cheeks.

'Hope couldn't say "blueberry" for a long time, and it kind of stuck, so now Evan makes her boobie pancakes at the weekend. Made,' she corrected. 'He made her boobie pancakes.'

Any humour or light-hearted relief the moment had offered them was gone, and Holly was about to apologise, even though she wasn't sure why. But before she could, Anne was speaking again.

'Well, why don't you let me take this little one and you go up and get an extra half an hour? How does that sound?'

Holly thought about it for a moment. It was definitely a tempting offer to go back to bed, but then what? She could risk a repeat of the previous day. No, what she needed was to be as active as possible, and hope that meant she could sleep better that evening.

'You know what? I think it's best if I push through,' Holly said. 'Besides, there's lots we want to see today, isn't there, Hope? As long as you're still okay to show us around,' she added.

'Of course,' Anne said, before looking back at Hope. 'Well, in that case, I better make enough boobie pancakes for all of us. And make sure you eat plenty. We've got a long walk planned for us today. One of Evvy's favourites, in fact.'

63

It was just the four of them that went to Evan's Creek Reserve: Holly, Hope, and Evan's parents. Holly didn't really know much about reserves. Was it a nature reserve or a heritage reserve? She felt like she should ask, perhaps, but then didn't want to appear ignorant. And so she stayed quiet until they parked up in the small parking lot.

'If you've brought your cell phone, make sure you leave it in the car,' Jonathan said, as Holly grabbed Hope out of the back seat. 'We have a rule here: no cells. We are with nature and each other and that's it.'

It was a lovely idea, one Holly would like to implement when she went on walks back home. That was her first thought. Her second was that it didn't feel quite right to be wandering down random footpaths without some way of contacting people if you found yourself in an emergency. Still, she didn't say as much. She was sure Jonathan knew what he was doing. Particularly if he'd been walking these trails since before Evan was born.

'Next time, you'll have to come in the spring,' Anne said to her. 'It's absolutely beautiful then. Not that it's not pretty now, but my goodness, the purple lupins by the walkway are absolutely stunning.'

Holly didn't doubt it. She looked out at the great expanse in front of her, in awe of just how enormous the place must be. Beautiful, long grasses, browned by winter, waved lazily in the breeze as a light wooden walkway cut over marshland.

'So you really named him after this place?' she said.

'We did. We used to come here walking all the time, and that was no easy feat, believe me. Not when I was expecting triplets, but they've got lovely paths here and Jonathan could push a double stroller with Ashley and Melissa in, and Catherine walked. She was tired by the end, but she didn't complain. And every time we came here, we always felt so connected to the place. We didn't know whether the triplets were going to be boys or girls, but when we had the one boy, it just seemed the most natural name to choose.'

Holly wanted to breathe it all in, breathe in this part of Evan she had never known. 'He used to come here too, I assume. You brought him and the triplets when they were older?'

'Oh yes, wasn't that an adventure? I mean, I told you about the cakes, right? Oh, the three of them were hard work. I mean, they stuck together. But they were always running off, holding hands, and you could guarantee it was in the opposite direction to Melissa and Ashley. And poor Catherine. She was such a good girl, trying to help me keep everyone safe, but it was like trying to herd cats. I used to come back after what was supposed to be a thirty-minute stroll feeling like I'd run an entire marathon. And each time, I'd swear it was the last. But what I wouldn't give to do it all again, just once.'

Holly knew exactly what she meant. She only had Hope, and she was still little, but already she could feel there were so many things slipping away from her, like how long would it be before

Hope was too heavy to sit on Holly's hip while she was baking, or no longer let them say boobie pancakes? How long would it be before she no longer needed Holly to put on her socks or help her wash her hair? There were so many firsts as a parent, and so many lasts, but while you recorded all those first moments with fervour and pride, you never realised when the last ones were happening, and before you knew it, they were a piece of history.

'Well, there are three different length trails we can do,' Anne said, as they carried on walking. 'But we'll see what you feel up to. I packed us a picnic, and as the weather's nice, I thought we could just stay out as long as it holds and Hope's happy.'

'That sounds perfect,' Holly said. Outside air felt like exactly what she needed, particularly this outside air. It was so fresh and crisp, it was like drinking ice water.

It was only when Hope was playing a game of chase with Jonathan that she realised she hadn't really asked him how he was doing. She'd spent so much time talking to Anne about Evan, learning about how she was feeling, she hadn't really thought about how this must be affecting Jonathan. After all, Evan had been his only male companion in the family, and now he was gone.

'He seems like he's doing okay,' Holly said, a slight nod of her head gesturing towards Jonathan. 'I take it he's not. How is he?'

'Honestly, I think us coming back here now has been a bit of a godsend to him. I can't imagine how he would have found it if I'd stayed in England with you and he'd been on his own with the girls. It makes me feel rather sick to think about, if I'm honest.'

Holly looked ahead to where Jonathan was currently jumping out at Hope, pretending to be a lion. He certainly didn't look like a father who was grieving his son.

'If I'm honest, I think it will hit him after the funeral,' Anne said. 'You know, when we're back here. It'll probably hit all of us then.'

Holly allowed the thought to flicker into her mind. The idea of laying Evan to rest was so final. That would be it. Life would move on. People would expect her to start rebuilding things. She would probably need to put the house on the market as there was no point paying such a hefty mortgage for just Hope and her. Maybe she could see if Giles would rent her the cottage again, she considered, letting the thoughts run away with her. Maybe it would be easiest for Hope being back in Bourton, close to everyone. Maybe it would be as if Evan had never existed for her.

The moment the thought formed, a searing heat spread out through Holly's chest. She clamped it down, using every bit of strength she had to quash it. With a deep breath in, she looked up at Anne, only to find her staring intently with an almost worried look in her eye.

'Anne? Is everything okay?'

Anne nodded. 'I know I shouldn't ask this, Holly,' Anne said, pausing before she carried on. 'You've already done so much, coming here, bringing Hope to us, but I wanted to ask you for one last favour before you leave. And I do hope you'll say yes.'

64

There was something about the way Anne was staring at Holly that made her certain this wasn't a small thing she wanted her to do, like come on a walk to Evan's favourite place, or watch old school performances with her.

'Of course,' Holly said, wishing she didn't feel obliged to give that answer before she'd actually heard what it was Anne wanted.

'I want us to have a memorial here for Evan before you leave,' she said. 'Jonathan and I are coming to the funeral, obviously, and Ashley will come over too, but it's difficult for Catherine with the children and Blake, so I don't think she can make it. And Emily doesn't want to fly, being pregnant and everything. Melissa will try, I know that, but work can be funny and as for Erin—'

'Sorry, Emily's pregnant?' Holly said, her jaw dropping open in surprise. How had she missed that?

Anne's cheeks turned fluorescent pink.

'I'm sorry, I know. She didn't want me to say anything. She only told the girls this week. It's early days and it's been quite a tough journey for her and her boyfriend to get this far. I know that flying would be fine, but we don't want to put her under any unnecessary stress, and I think she'd find the funeral too hard. Not to mention the travelling.'

Holly understood. She was barely coping with the jet lag as it was. She couldn't imagine handling it with morning sickness on top.

'I get it,' Holly said. 'Yes, of course, I understand. That makes sense.'

'About the memorial, you mean?'

Holly hadn't meant that at all. She had been thinking purely about Emily not travelling. But she nodded anyway. Her throat tickled a little as if it didn't want her to say any more, but she knew she had to. For Anne and Jonathan.

'Evan grew up here,' she said. 'Of course, you want to have a memorial for him.'

Anne nodded, and a brief, weak smile formed on her lips before it disappeared again.

'Several of the neighbours have already asked, you see. And some school friends. I just... I hoped you might do a small speech, you know. A eulogy for him.'

'You want me to speak?' Holly asked.

A ripple of tension gripped her shoulders and neck. Holly didn't do speeches. She was not that type of person. In fact, the only time she'd done one since school was at a charity fundraiser in Bourton, and it had terrified her. And that was a very different event. There, she had known what she was talking about. And it had been for charity. But here, she would be talking to people who had known Evan for decades more than she had. What could she possibly have to say about him that they didn't already know?

'That's a very lovely offer,' Holly said, trying not to sound ungrateful. 'But I'm sure there are people who are better suited to it. Emily or Erin?'

Anne nodded, but it wasn't the type of nod of someone who

was agreeing with what was being said; it was the rapid nod of someone who was trying to think through what they were going to say next.

'Emily will say something, yes. I've already asked her. And as for Erin, well, let's be honest, we don't even know if she'll turn up, but you're the one who's lived with Evan these last years. Who's renovated a house with him. You're the one who loved him enough to want to spend the rest of your life with him.'

Anne glanced down at Holly's hand, at the ring Holly refused to take off.

Holly knew how much this would mean to Anne, and it wasn't that she didn't want to do it. She just didn't know if she could. Maybe if she had one of her friends with her and she wasn't going to be surrounded by people she barely knew, it would have been okay. Maybe if Ben hadn't had to go, and she didn't feel quite so alone, then a very short speech would have been something she could have managed. But, no. No was the answer that Holly wanted to say. Sorry, she understood, but it wasn't something she could do.

The answer was there on the tip of her tongue when she looked forward and saw Jonathan hoisting Hope up into a fireman's lift. And she knew there was only one thing she could say.

'Okay, yes. I'll say something. It doesn't have to be long, though, does it?' She could already feel the anxiety taking hold.

'Whatever you can manage,' Anne said. With a visible sigh of relief, Anne slipped her arm back into Holly's. 'Thank you,' Anne continued. 'And since I'm already asking you to do things you don't feel comfortable with, I wondered if you might come somewhere with me tomorrow, too?'

65

Thankfully, Anne's next request wasn't anywhere near as bad as having to say a piece at Evan's memorial. Instead, she wanted Holly to come Christmas shopping with her the following day. Although it wasn't just her. It was all the women in Evan's family. Including Erin.

'It's a big tradition,' she says. 'All us girls go out shopping, enjoying the Christmas lights and a glass of eggnog, while Evan and his dad go out and chop down a tree.'

At this, Anne's words faded, and Holly could see the pain forming in her eyes.

'That part of the tradition will have to change a bit now, I suppose. You know, in all his life, he only missed cutting down the tree with his dad three times. I suppose that's something we should be grateful for.'

Holly could feel all the joy Anne had felt mentioning the girls' shopping trip, slipping away from them. So she said the first thing she could think of to try to stop that from happening.

'Perhaps we could do the tree this evening?' Holly suggested. 'I know it's not tradition, but maybe Hope and I could come. I'm sure Jonathan would like that.'

Anne nodded, but she smiled tightly. 'That's a lovely offer, Holly. Really it is, but I think maybe we can do without a tree this year. I don't think anyone will be in the mood to decorate it. To be honest, if it wasn't for Hope and the other grandchildren, I'm not sure I'd want to go Christmas shopping either, but Evan would want us to keep up with these things, wouldn't he? That's what he would want, so that's what we are going to do.'

Holly couldn't help but stare at Anne with a look of wonder and disbelief. How was she holding it all together? If anything happened to Hope, that would be it. She couldn't imagine how she would ever get out of bed. Right now, Hope was the one thing that was helping her get through the day. Maybe that was why Anne was coping so well. On the outside, at least. She still had five other children to think of, not to mention five grandchildren and another on the way.

An unexpected pang struck in Holly's chest. She and Evan had always talked about having more children. It had never been an if, but always a when. She hadn't wanted Hope to be an only child, and while she knew Evan loved Hope like his own, she wanted him to go through the full experience with her, too. But now that would never happen. It would just be her and Hope, alone. Always.

'Holly, hon, are you okay?'

It was only feeling Anne's hand on Holly's shoulder that made Holly realise she'd slumped forwards.

'Yes, yes, I'm fine,' she said, straightening herself out. 'Just tired, I think.'

'Of course. We've been out for a long time, and you didn't get much sleep, did you? We should get you home.'

Holly was about to reply that heading back sounded like a

good idea when she thought about what awaited her back at the house. Memories of Evan. That was it. Memories of Evan and a speech she had to write about how he was gone. The past and the pain were all that awaited her there.

While up ahead, Jonathan and Hope were now sitting on a bench, sharing a bag of crisps and as thick as thieves.

'Let's keep going a little longer,' she said.

66

It was another two hours before they got back to the car, by which point Hope was well and truly exhausted. She flopped against Jonathan's shoulder as he carried her and carefully placed her in the car seat.

'A quick nap will probably be a good idea,' Holly said, 'though I'll have to wake her up when she gets back to the house. I don't really want her having more than that. She'll be up all night otherwise.'

'You can always send her into us,' Anne suggested. 'I'll be awake.'

Holly didn't doubt that it was true, and the words sparked a level of concern.

'I hope you don't think I'm out of line,' Holly said, wondering if it was her place to broach the subject, 'but have you thought about going to the doctor to get something to help you sleep? You don't have to take them forever, just until your body finds its rhythm.'

Anne shook her head and let out a slight laugh.

'Now you really are sounding like one of my girls with all your fussing,' she said. 'I was never much of a sleeper before. A busy mind, you know. But maybe I'll think about it.'

Holly had the distinct impression that this was what Anne had said to her daughters too, brushing away the comment with no actual intention of taking the advice, but Holly wasn't going to press the matter. It wasn't her place. Like Anne said, she had plenty of actual family members to do that.

Holly's desire that Hope didn't nap for too long was assured when she woke up the moment they clipped the car seat around her.

'Mamma?' Hope said.

'Hey, you,' Holly replied, kissing her daughter on the forehead. 'That wasn't a long sleep, was it?'

'Walk? Go walk?' Hope said, pointing out of the window.

'Not now. We've finished walking,' Holly replied. 'We're going back to the house.'

A deep frown crinkled Hope's forehead, before suddenly disappearing and being replaced with a look of delight.

'And play Lolly?' Hope said. 'Hope play Lolly?'

The love between the cousins was clearly mutual and Holly was about to ask Evan's parents if they knew whether Melissa had plans for that afternoon when Anne spoke.

'That's funny,' she said as she sat in the passenger seat, staring at her phone.

'What is it?' Jonathan asked.

'Just a lot of missed calls from an unknown number. Probably someone who's heard about Evan and wants to know about the memorial. I'll call them when I get back.'

Holly found her heart hurting at the comment. How many times had Anne had to tell someone her son had died? she wondered. How many pitying phone calls had she been made to suffer from well-meaning people? Worse still, how many people wouldn't know? For how many years would people casually slip his name into conversation as if he was still around? Holly's mind flipped to the sweet shop. What had Caroline and Drey been telling customers who asked where Holly was? Had they told them the truth? If so, how many sorrowful, pity-filled looks would be awaiting her when she got back? But, Holly considered, if they hadn't, then she would have to tell them herself, and that would be even worse.

'I'll put the arrangements together tonight,' Anne said, still talking to Jonathan. 'Mel messaged and said they've all headed to the mall to do a bit of a shop. They'll grab takeout for dinner, if you're okay with that?' She twisted around to look at Holly as she said the last question. 'You don't mind takeout, do you?' she asked.

Holly shook her head. 'Sounds good.'

Rather than turning back around and facing the front again, Anne remained looking at Holly for just a moment longer.

'It's strange to think we're all going to be back on a flight to England in a few days and getting ready for the funeral. It feels like you've only just got here,' she said.

'I know,' Holly replied.

The comment caused them to fall into silence. In three days, Holly would be back on a flight to the UK with Evan's family set to follow soon after. It wouldn't be long before she'd be back in the sweet shop, and expected to just go on with life. But then she knew that already, didn't she? That was why it had been so important to make this trip and say goodbye to Evan in a positive way. So why did it make her feel so uneasy?

Silence filled the car, and the rumble of the engine became the background sound to their thoughts. As Holly stared out of the window, she began to understand why tired toddlers and babies fell asleep in cars so easily. While Hope was once again wide awake, she could feel her eyes lulling her from the gentle motion.

Two minutes into the trip and her chin was repeatedly dropping onto her chest.

'Who the heck do you think that is?'

Holly hadn't realised she had fallen asleep until Jonathan's voice woke her up. They were already on the driveway, headed back to the house, though the car was crawling at a peculiarly slow speed, as Jonathan peered out the side window, clearly looking for something.

'Did you see him?' Jonathan asked. 'Why's he standing outside our door with a suitcase?'

Holly's gaze moved through the window, where she tried to see who it was. Unfortunately, Hope was on that side of the car, and there was the added obstruction of trees blocking her view. Not that she expected to have any idea who was standing at Anne and Jonathan's front door. It was most likely to be an old school friend of Evan's or perhaps one of the girls' boyfriends, although she thought Jonathan would probably recognise those people.

Holly slumped back into the seat, allowing herself an indulgently long yawn when Hope let out a squeal of delight.

'Uncle Giles!' she said.

67

Holly blinked a couple of times. In her sleepy state, she was sure she must have heard Hope incorrectly. After all, she wasn't always the most eloquent – boobie pancakes was proof of that. Yet she was bouncing in the car seat and waving madly out of the window with a look of pure delight on her face.

'Mamma! Uncle Giles!' she said again.

The car was moving towards the garage now, offering a clear view of the front of the house. Holly's heart hammered against her ribs as she held her breath. It couldn't be. It wasn't possible, and yet there he was.

'Is that…'

Holly didn't finish her sentence. There was no mistaking him. There, standing on Anne and Jonathan's doorstep, with a leather bag, looking notably dishevelled, was Giles Caverty.

As Jonathan drew the car to a stop, Holly pinged off her belt.

'Anne, can you get Hope?' Holly said, already opening the door and leaping from the vehicle. She didn't wait to hear Anne's reply as she rushed towards the house. Several feet away from Giles, she stopped.

'What are you doing?' she said. There was still a substantial distance between the pair, but Holly didn't want to get any closer. Not in case it was all part of her imagination. Hadn't she been thinking only a couple of hours ago, when Anne had asked her to speak at the memorial, that she needed one of her friends here? Hadn't that been the thought going around in Holly's head? She remembered the feeling, too. That ache spreading out beneath her sternum. All she'd wanted was someone whose hand she could hold without feeling the need to speak or act a certain way. And here he was, standing in front of her.

'What are you doing here, Giles?' she repeated, not even sure her voice was loud enough to reach him.

Without a word, Giles placed his bag down on the path and walked towards her.

'Well, it turns out I was the only one who could take the time off work, so I'm the one you're stuck with.'

'You're here for me?'

'Why else would I be here?'

Holly stepped forward, not sure if she wanted to laugh or cry. No doubt Ben had had a hand in it too. He probably rang Giles, feeling guilty about having to leave Holly and Hope so suddenly. Not that he had anything to feel guilty about. Still, whoever was responsible for the logistics, it was ridiculous. Giles had travelled all this way, just to be with her for a couple of days. She knew she should have been cross with him for doing something so ridiculous, but she could barely speak at all.

In the end, it was Hope who broke the silence.

'Uncle Giles!' she said, before running straight at him and leaping into his arms.

'Hey, trouble,' Giles said, lifting her up and spinning her in the air. 'Did you miss me?'

68

Several minutes of fussing followed, during which Giles explained he had already booked a hotel room, just a short way away, but Anne wasn't having any of it.

'You haven't travelled all this way to be with Holly and stay in a soulless hotel. No, you're staying here. Besides, you're a friend of Evan's, too, and he would want you to stay here with us.'

Holly may not have known Anne that long, but she knew her well enough to know that she wasn't going to take no for an answer.

'Come on,' Holly said to Giles, picking up his bag. 'I'll show you to the office where Ben was sleeping. Assuming that's okay, Anne?'

'Yes, yes, absolutely. And let me know if there's anything else I can get you,' Anne said. 'There's a heater in that room and plenty of blankets, but if you need any more, just let me know.'

'Thank you, but this is already more than enough,' Giles said.

While Hope stayed with her grandparents, Holly led Giles through the house to the office. She could already hear Hope asking for Lolly, but Holly was grateful the rest of the family was out. She wasn't sure how Giles would have explained turning up on the doorstep if they'd been the ones to answer.

'You know, you really didn't need to come,' Holly said as they reached the office. 'It's not that I don't appreciate it, but I would have been fine without you.'

'That's what worried me,' Giles replied.

Holly frowned. 'What does that mean?'

'It means you're not giving yourself any time at all. Rushing around like this. I'm just worried about you. We all are.'

At least that confirmed one thing. This hadn't been a decision Giles had made on his own. The others had clearly been discussing her state of mind in her absence. She would bet money on the fact that both her parents knew Giles was out here, too.

Holly drew in a long, deep breath and let it out slowly. As much as it irritated her, she knew there was no point in getting angry with him. With any of them. They were just trying to help.

'Well, you don't need to be worried,' she said. 'I'm doing okay. All things considered. It's not exactly easy, but I'm doing okay.'

'And the family? How are they holding up?'

Holly filled Giles in on everything that had happened so far, from how much Hope had fallen in love with everyone, to the way Holly had yelled at Catherine's son at the lake then blown up at Erin at the dining table only a couple of hours later.

'Trust me, I'm not holding it together half as well as I appear to be,' she said. 'I feel like I'm teetering on a ledge the whole time and no matter how much I try to get my footing, all it's going to take is one thing to send me careening off the edge.'

'Then maybe you need to let it?' Giles replied.

'What's that meant to mean?'

Giles reached out and took Holly's hand. 'It means that you don't have to hold it together. Not all the time. Not around people who love you. If you need to yell at someone, or smash a few plates, then that's okay.'

'Smash a few plates?' Holly said, raising an eyebrow.

'It's just a suggestion.'

She released a light chuckle that faded into the air. It sounded great. To let it all go. To scream aloud and yell at the world the way she had done to Erin. But acting like that had repercussions and how did it help anyone in the long run, when all you were really doing was causing more hurt? She didn't want to be that person. Evan would never have expected her to become that person.

'Anne wants me to go on the girls' family Christmas shopping trip tomorrow,' Holly continued, 'before doing a speech at a memorial she's arranging for Tuesday. I mean, what am I supposed to say? They all knew Evan his entire life. They know him far better than I did.'

'I don't think that will be true at all,' Giles said. 'And I'm sure Anne's not expecting you to stand up there and do a thirty-minute monologue. Just say what Evan meant to you and Hope, that's all.'

Holly thought about his words for a moment, only to discover they held the simplest answer of all.

'He was everything,' she said.

Giles nodded. 'I know. And if I could trade places with him, in a heartbeat, I would – you know that. I'd do anything for him to be here now for you.'

Holly didn't have the strength to reply. What could she say to something like that? To someone wanting to trade places with the person she lost? Then again, maybe that's what any friend would have wanted for her.

'Giles—' Holly started, but before she could continue, he was speaking again.

'And as for the shopping tomorrow, that sounds like a good idea. It might give you a chance to talk things through with this

Erin a bit more. And don't worry about Hope. She and I are due a full day together, I think.'

For the first time since they had started talking, Holly's thoughts were well and truly distracted from Evan. Sure, Giles had looked after Hope for half an hour or so, plenty of times. Like times when he'd popped over to theirs and Holly had realised she needed to run down to the shop. Or when he'd taken her out to feed the ducks when they were at the pub, so Evan and Holly could enjoy chatting with the others. Holly knew Giles was capable of looking after Hope for small quantities of time. But for a whole day?

'Don't look at me like that,' he said, reading Holly's expression perfectly. 'We'll have fun, I promise. Besides, you'd let Fin and Michael look after her for a day.'

'True,' Holly agreed. 'But Michael has children and Fin's... well, Fin.'

However insulted Giles could have been by the comment, he didn't show it. Instead, he just puffed out his chest and grinned.

'Well, I'm Giles, and I'm telling you that Hope and I will be absolutely fine. Trust me, you are going shopping with the girls.'

69

'Are you sure you've got everything you need? You know you can call me, right? If you need anything, just call me.'

Holly had spent the night tossing and turning, thinking of a hundred reasons why she didn't want to go shopping with Anne or speak at the memorial. Yet morning arrived and she had somehow been swept into the moment and now she was giving Giles a list, which mainly included making sure that Hope had enough to eat and not too much screen time, but she still wanted to double-check everything with him one last time.

'Holly, I'm fine, honestly,' he groaned. 'Will you please just go?'

'We do need to get going, Holly,' Ashley said, placing her hand on Holly's shoulder. 'Catherine and Mel have already left and I've told everyone we're meeting at nine thirty. We always get dough-nuts before we start the shop. If we don't go now, the queue will be crazy.'

Holly nodded. 'Right, yes, of course.' She turned back to Giles. 'Just—'

'I will ring if I need anything.' Giles sighed. 'Unless you don't leave now – in that case, I won't. Hope, give your mummy a big kiss. You and I are going to have a day filled with age-inappro-priate adventures that we'll tell her nothing about.'

'Giles...' Holly said worriedly.

'Sorry. Just go. Okay? We'll speak soon.'

'Thank you. Love you, Hopey,' Holly said, giving Hope one last kiss before she headed outside.

'How's Mum doing?' Ashley whispered as they walked towards the car. 'Is she holding up okay? I stayed at Emily's last night as Mum said she was fine. She said she didn't want the house over-filled, with your friend being here, but I think she's just avoiding seeing us, you know? I think somehow, we make it harder.'

Holly slowed her pace. They were only a few feet from the car and it was likely that any second, Anne would call them and ask what they were talking about. After all Evan's mother had done for her, the last thing Holly wanted to do was talk about her behind her back, but she had to agree with Ashley.

'I think she's blocking it all out. She says she's worried about how your dad is going to cope after the funeral, but she hasn't stopped since we got here. And I don't think she's sleeping either. I wish there was something I could do to help.'

'Trust me, you being here is helping,' Ashley said, echoing the same words Anne had said to her only the day before. 'We're all really grateful, you know.'

There was something about her use of the word 'all' that caused Holly to flinch a little. It didn't feel like all of them were grateful at all.

'How's Erin doing?' Holly said, knowing she couldn't avoid the point forever, not when they were about to go shopping together. 'I know she's hurting.'

'We all are. I'll be honest, Erin's always been one for drama, but this is odd. She's not picking up any calls. The only person she'll speak to is Em, and it doesn't sound like she's telling her the entire story either. I'm not even sure she's going to come today.'

This last part left Holly surprised. From the way Anne had spoken, Christmas shopping sounded like a tradition they did every year. Something that meant a lot to her. Still, she couldn't help but feel a flicker of relief at the thought of Erin being absent from the day. It would certainly make it more pleasant for her. Not that she was going to say that to Ashley.

'Come on, girls!' Anne called from the front of the car. 'What are you dawdling for? We'll miss the doughnuts if you don't hurry up.'

70

Ashley was right about two things: the first being that the doughnuts were incredible, and the second, that Erin wouldn't show.

They had been waiting at the meeting point for twenty minutes before Catherine called it.

'She can message us if she wants to know where we are and join us,' she said. 'I need to get to the shops. I haven't bought Parker a single thing yet. This was my scheduled day for shopping.'

'Same,' Melissa agreed. 'Tomorrow is the last day I've booked off work, and I can hardly go shopping then, because it's well, you know.'

Evan's memorial. That was what she couldn't say. And she didn't need to say it. They all knew.

'Okay,' Ashley said, clapping her hands together with forced positivity. 'Then I guess we'd better get going.'

* * *

As strained as the beginning of the day had been, the rest of it was far more pleasant than Holly had imagined. She had bought far more than she had planned, with gifts for Hope and Caroline's children, not to mention an exceptionally cute, cuddly toy for Jamie's baby, whenever they arrived.

They talked about previous Christmases, presents they had all got, mishaps with meals and gifts. They spoke about Evan freely, and Holly got the impression that this was commonplace on these trips. That every year, they would speak this way and reminisce. Probably even more so since Evan had moved away.

It would be easier for Evan's sisters, Holly thought as she stared into her cup of eggnog. It would be easier for them because, while Evan was part of their lives, he wasn't their life. They didn't wake up next to him each morning, or spend their evenings curled up with their head on his shoulder. He wasn't the first person they called for anything, or the first one they thought of when anything happened during the day. He was part of their life, but he wasn't their life. And what did it mean when you no longer had that person who made up your entire world?

'Excuse me,' Holly said, finding the sudden heat of the coffee shop overwhelming. 'I think I need to get some air.'

'Are you okay?' Ashley was on her feet, but Holly waved her concern away.

'Yes, absolutely. Please, stay. I'll just be a second.'

Before they could protest any more, she slipped outside.

It was only when the cold air stung her skin that Holly realised she'd left her coat hanging on the back of the chair, with her gloves in the pocket.

She rubbed her hands together and blew on them, her warm breath forming clouds of condensation in the air. The sudden shock from the drop in temperature was enough to push thoughts of Evan from her mind for just a moment as she stared across at the cityscape. It was a long way from Bourton High Street and the Cotswolds, that was for sure. Cars travelled slowly down the road, at barely a walking pace, while three- or four-storey buildings with their square shopfronts looked out onto the road. Seattle was far prettier than Holly had imagined, with large trees, likely hundreds of years old, lining the road. It was clear she and Evan's family weren't the only ones using the day for shopping. Hundreds of people bustled about, wrapped up warm with hats and scarves, arms laden with bags. Holly would have liked to have watched them for longer, imagining their stories, but she was shivering now and about to head back inside when a particular person caught Holly's eye. They weren't moving around like everyone else but were on their own, on the other side of the road, and appeared to be looking straight at her.

After a second, Holly was sure about it. They were staring straight at her. And she knew exactly who it was.

Erin.

71

Holly didn't know what she was hoping to achieve, but before she could stop herself, she was marching across the road, barely aware of the traffic. She was sure that at any moment, Erin was going to bolt. To run away. And Holly wasn't going to have that. If Erin had something to say to her again, then she could say it to her face, here, alone, away from the rest of her family.

Every step closer, Holly was sure Erin was going to turn around and race away, but she didn't, and it was only when Holly was halfway across the road, she realised she wasn't going to. This was it. Whatever Erin wanted to say was going to be said, here and now.

Holly's heart drummed in her chest, a fire burning within her that set her mind whirring. She would let Erin say whatever it was she felt she had to, and then she would offer her a few home truths straight back. Holly planned on letting Erin know exactly how pathetic her behaviour was. How hurtful she was being to her parents when Anne and Jonathan were already in so much pain. She would let her know how embarrassed and ashamed for her Evan would be and how disappointed she was that the sister he had talked about with nothing but love and admiration turned out to be a spoilt, selfish child.

Holly was fired up for a fight, ready to give it all she got. Only when she reached Erin, she stopped.

Like everybody else on the street except Holly, Erin was dressed in a scarf and hat, the latter of which tied up around her chin. Yet it was still easy to see how her face was streaked with tears. Her eyes were sunken in and grey, while her cheeks and nose were bright red, as if she had spent hours out in the cold.

'Have you been following us all day?' Holly said, realising the reason for Erin's appearance. 'You didn't join everyone because of me? Is that why? I didn't ask to join, you know. Anne wanted me to. Anne wanted us all to be together, you included. If you'd have just said you wanted this to be for you and your sisters, I would have understood. I would have stayed away. But you can't come here now, claiming I'm the villain, when I've done everything I can to make everyone here as happy as possible. I just don't get what it is you want from me.'

Holly knew she hadn't given Erin a chance to speak – the exact opposite of what she had intended to do – but once she'd started, it had been near impossible to stop. Now, though, as silence swelled around them, she wished she'd just stayed quiet.

Holly waited, the cold now stinging her lips and ears, and she was one second away from turning around and heading back into the coffee shop when Erin spoke.

'Can we go somewhere to talk?' she asked. 'Just the two of us?'

72

Holly messaged Anne, saying she would be back in twenty. She apologised and mentioned finding a shop where she wanted to get something for Hope. She knew they would all think she was lying, and that was okay, because she didn't want to tell them the truth. Not yet. Not when she wasn't even sure what the truth was. What Erin wanted to say to her.

Erin led Holly into a coffee shop just a short walk away, though by the time they got there, her fingers were throbbing from the cold.

'I'll get us eggnogs,' Erin said, but Holly shook her head.

'A water will be fine,' she said. 'I just had a drink with your family.'

Erin nodded, then disappeared to order. When she came back, she had two glasses of water and two hot chocolates.

'You're cold,' she said. 'You can just hold it to warm up your hands if you want. I don't really care if you drink it or not.'

It was a kind gesture, but wrapped in the most peculiar manner. Never had Holly struggled to read someone as much as she was struggling to read Erin. At that moment, it was almost as if

Erin was trying to make Holly like her, which was very different from before.

'Why didn't you come shopping?' Holly said, deciding there was no point beating around the bush with false niceties if they were just going to end up shouting at one another again. 'Your mum wanted you there. She was upset. She hid it well, but she was upset.'

Erin nodded as if she knew this was the case, but then Holly suspected it wasn't chance that she'd been standing outside the coffee shop. While she didn't know for certain, Holly suspected Erin had been there all day. Right from the early-morning doughnuts, watching them. Keeping herself apart.

'He sent us pictures of the ring, you know,' she said instead. 'Actually, he sent us loads of rings and asked us which one. I think he went with Ashley's choice, but I can't say I know for sure.'

'Really?' Holly said, not sure how she was supposed to reply. She didn't want to make out that the other sisters had already told her this, not when Erin was obviously trying to build some bridges, but the whole thing still felt so off. 'Which one did you pick?'

'I didn't. I didn't respond to those messages.'

Holly's stomach dropped. Any hope she'd had that this was going to be a reconciliation was drastically slipping away. Yet before she could ask again what Erin wanted to talk to her about, Erin was speaking again.

'I hadn't spoken to Evan in three months. It's the longest we've ever gone in our lives without speaking, and that's it. It's done. There's nothing I can do to go back. I was being a bitch and wasn't speaking to him, and now he's dead, and there's nothing I can do about it.'

73

Holly was stunned into silence. Suddenly, it made sense why Erin had been so angry this whole time. She wasn't angry with Holly. She was angry with herself.

'What happened?' Holly asked, amazed that she was only just hearing about this now. 'Evan didn't say anything.'

'No, it doesn't surprise me,' Erin replied. 'He probably thought it was just one of my spats, and that the next time I saw him, everything would be good, and he was probably right. Only there wasn't a next time, was there? The last words I said to him were "screw you", or something to that effect. I can't even remember exactly. You'd think I'd be able to, right? You'd think I'd be able to remember the last words I said to my brother?'

Tears were falling down Erin's cheeks, and Holly wanted nothing more than to wipe them away, but she couldn't.

'I'll be one minute,' Holly said instead. Erin looked up, probably expecting Holly to move, only she didn't. She was still sitting right there, and had no intention of moving either. 'I'll be one minute. Those were the last words I said to him. I just think about them over and over. Just how if I hadn't said them, if I hadn't left him at that moment, then maybe... maybe there would have been something I could have done.'

'There wouldn't have been,' Erin said immediately.

'There might have been.'

Erin shook her head. 'No, his body was already shutting down. You couldn't have done anything. I know you couldn't.'

Holly knew it was true. The paramedics and doctors had said as much to her, but it still didn't make the guilt any less.

'What did you fight about?' Holly asked. She didn't mean to pry; it was just that she couldn't imagine Evan ever being the person who would upset someone so much, they would stop speaking to him.

'I needed some money,' Erin said.

Everyone knew that generally speaking, money was one of the most common causes of family disputes, yet Holly couldn't imagine Evan's family falling out over such a thing. Just like she couldn't imagine Evan not helping his sister out if she was truly in need. She wanted to say as much, but she didn't know how to express such a thing without coming across as callous. As it happened, she didn't need to.

'There was an art studio I wanted to purchase. It had a gallery attached, and I had this whole vision of this community space, with different—' Erin shook her head, stopping before she had even finished the sentence. 'It doesn't matter. I asked Evan to come and look at it with me, to invest. He said he would, saw the place, and said it wasn't a viable business option. He wouldn't lend me the money because it wouldn't be sustainable.'

'If that's what he told you, I'm sure he was right,' Holly said, not wanting to add tension to the situation, yet feeling the need to defend Evan. 'He was the most business-savvy person I know.'

'I know. I do. I think that's why I was so mad,' Erin said. 'I just got my hopes so high, you know, and I blamed him for it not happening. Of course, it wasn't him. He was the most generous person I ever met. You know, he paid for everything during Catherine's divorce and settled Mum and Dad's house the minute he could afford to. But I was hurt. I didn't see it as a business decision. It felt personal. Like he didn't believe in me.'

'Evan believed in you, 100 per cent. I know that. I know how proud he was of you. Of all of you. He always talked about you.'

A sad smile flickered on Erin's face. It was the first smile she'd managed in Holly's presence and it caused a deep tug in Holly's chest. It all made sense now. The comments about how Holly had only wanted Evan for his money. Erin had been projecting all her pain onto Holly.

'You know, before we saw the building and I got mad, we were talking about getting tattoos the next time he came over. Me, Evan, and Em. It was something we always said we were going to do. I just feel like if we'd done that... If we'd had something tangible to hold us together...'

Holly knew exactly what Erin meant. She had her ring, of course, to link her to Evan, but he had never actually given it to her. Though she had never been a tattoo person, she could understand that having something etched into your skin, a permanent reminder of who he was, would be comforting, which was why a slight smile lifted on her lips.

'Let's do it then,' she said. 'Let's go get them. Let's get tattoos.'

74

'I don't think I want this to become a new family tradition,' Anne said as they walked in through the front door. They had all come back to the house together after the impromptu trip to the tattoo parlour. What had started out as Erin and Holly wanting this permanent reminder, turned into all the sisters, bar Emily, getting tattoos of the letter 'E' in various places on their bodies. Although Emily assured them that the moment the baby arrived happy and healthy, she, too, would do the same. Catherine chose to have the letter on her ankle and Ashley on her ribs, but Holly decided on her wrist, somewhere she would be able to see it all the time. Despite several attempts by all the sisters for their mother to join in, Anne had not been persuaded.

'Your father's not going to be happy about this, you know,' she said.

'What are you talking about? I bet he'll get one too,' Erin replied.

Holly thought about her own parents, what Arthur and Wendy's reaction might be, but the thought was quickly dismissed as she walked in towards the kitchen. She had a far more important person to catch up with.

'Hello, baby,' she said, as Hope rushed straight into her arms. 'How's your day been with Uncle Giles? Sorry I've been so long.'

'We've been fine, haven't we?' Giles said, stepping towards Holly and kissing her lightly on the cheek. 'We've had a wonderful day. We did lots of cooking and crafts and did you know that Grandad Jonathan has an air rifle? We've been playing with that too, haven't we, Hopey?'

Holly's jaw fell open. 'You have not,' she said.

'No, of course we haven't,' Giles said with a smirk. 'We have had a good day, though. We've been very calm. Hope taught me how to make shortbread. She knew the quantities and everything.'

'That's Mummy's girl. Are there still plenty for me to eat? I could do with some shortbread,' Holly said, only to realise they were standing in the kitchen doorway, and she had forgotten something very important.

'Sorry, everyone,' she said, turning to where Evan's family were crowded behind her. 'This is Giles. He's a friend from Bourton. He flew in to keep an eye on me when Ben had to leave. Not that I need it, but it was very sweet of him.'

'Hi, nice to meet everyone,' Giles said, flashing his normal, charming smile as he offered all five sisters a little wave.

'Holly's lucky to have so many generous people to look after her,' Erin said, obviously trying to make up for the remark she'd made about Ben previously. 'You'll have to make sure she comes back regularly, okay? Not that she has any choice now. We're bonded.'

Erin lifted her wrist to show it to Giles. She was the only person who had got her letter E in the same place as Holly, although they were very different in style. Erin had gone for a large, typewriter-type font, while Holly's was a more delicate script. Something subtle for her alone. All of the tattoos were still covered in the clear plastic film the tattoo parlour had wrapped them in, meaning there was no mistaking how fresh they were.

'Yes, this is why we were a little later back than expected,' Holly said, twisting her wrist around to show Giles hers. She looked up at him, expecting to see him sharing in her joy. After all, she felt lighter than she had done all week. But his face was thunderous.

'You got a tattoo?' he said. 'Please tell me you're joking?'

75

The atmosphere changed instantly. One minute, for the first time that Holly could recall, the girls had been all laughter and smiles and now everyone was silent, looking at one another awkwardly.

'We should put all this shopping in the dining room,' Ashley said, taking Erin by the hand and leading her away from the kitchen. 'We don't want the children to see it.'

With murmurs of agreement, the others quickly followed, although when Anne tried to take Hope, she wasn't going to go easily.

'Hope stay Mamma,' she said.

'You can see Mummy in a moment. Come with Nanny,' Anne said. But Hope wasn't moving. She was clinging to Holly's leg.

'Two minutes, Hopey,' Holly said, crouching down so she was at Hope's level. 'I'll be two minutes. Then I'm going to try that shortbread of yours, all right?'

Anne caught Holly's gaze before offering a brief nod, picking Hope up and disappearing after the rest of the family.

Holly stood back up, ready to give Giles a piece of her mind, but he got in there first.

'What on earth were you thinking?' he said. The rage in his face hadn't faded at all. If anything, he looked even more furious than before.

'What was I thinking?' Holly said, in near disbelief. 'What do you think I was thinking? I was thinking about Evan. About trying to remember him.'

'And you need to get a permeant tattoo to do that? Come on, Holly.'

Holly's face hardened. 'It's called grieving, Giles.'

Rather than responding immediately, Giles just shook his head.

'This is not grieving, Holly. You're not even processing what's happened. You're just running away from your problems and getting a tattoo to cover it up.'

'Excuse me?' She could feel her mouth hanging open in disbelief.

'It's true. Tell me, if Ben hadn't made you, would you have even told Hope why you were really here?' Holly's back teeth ground together. She should have known Ben wouldn't have kept something like that to himself. 'I haven't even seen you shed a single tear since I've been here.'

Holly was finding it all harder and harder to take in. 'What? So because I'm not a blubbering wreck, I'm not grieving? Trust me, Giles, I know exactly what I've lost.'

'Really? Then why aren't you at home facing it, with your friends and your family who need you?'

'Evan's family needs me, too.'

Giles scoffed and shook his head again. 'Surely you can see this isn't like you, Holly. Flying off to the other side of the world isn't like you. Getting a tattoo without even spending a day to think it over isn't like you. And what happens in a year's time, in ten years' time, when you don't want to be reminded of Evan constantly and he's there permanently scribbled on your wrist?'

Holly had heard enough.

'You think that's how it works?' Her voice was more like a low snarl than speech. 'You think in ten years' time, I'm just going to have forgotten about him?'

Giles let out a long sigh. 'That's not what I was saying. You know what I meant.'

'It sounded like that's what you were saying,' Holly said. She felt the same as she had during her fight with Erin. She hadn't been the one to start it, but she was sure as hell going to be the one who finished it.

Her eyes narrowed on her opponent.

'Why did you even come here, Giles? What were you hoping to achieve? You wanted to be the one to comfort me? How gallant of you. You're such a good friend. Or maybe you were hoping to slip into Evan's place, now that he's gone? Maybe you thought you'd finally got a chance with me.'

She watched as the colour drained from Giles's cheeks.

'I would never do that.'

'Well, the shoe certainly fits, doesn't it? Maybe you came here hoping to find me all weak and helpless, so that you could put me back together, and I'd be forever grateful. No wonder you're so mad about the tattoo. You were always hoping it was your name I'd get.'

Holly's heart continued to pound, and she was almost breathless as she waited for Giles's response. Whatever he said, she would go for him. She wasn't backing down. But rather than speaking, Giles remained where he was, completely silent. When he looked up at Holly, there was no anger left in his face. From what she could tell, there was no emotion at all.

'I think it's best if I leave now,' he said. 'I've still got the room booked at the hotel. I'll see you on the plane back.'

Without another word, he reached up, grabbed his coat from the coat stand and walked out of the door.

76

Holly felt undeniably embarrassed as she headed into the dining room.

'I guess you guys heard all of that,' she said.

'Not everything,' Catherine tried, but the others looked at her and raised their eyebrows.

'Yes, we heard everything,' Ashley said. 'Are you okay? Sounds like some pretty harsh words were said there.'

'Honestly, it's fine,' Holly said. 'I don't even know why he turned up here. Really. It's fine.' She tried to smile, but her cheeks didn't move quite the way she had hoped they would. She let them fall back down. 'I guess today has taken it out of me a little more than I thought it would. I should probably get Hope in the bath.'

As always, Hope was listening in on every word, and what Holly had just said left her less than pleased.

'Shortbread, Mamma,' she said, with a stamp of her foot. 'Mamma, eat shortbread.'

'Of course, of course,' Holly said. 'You're right.'

She reached down, ready to pick Hope up, take her into the kitchen and dutifully eat one of the aforementioned biscuits before heading upstairs and disappearing for the evening, to save from any further embarrassment. But before she could, Anne was on her feet, talking directly to Hope.

'Hope, sweetie,' Anne said. 'Why don't you get everyone sitting where you want, and I'll go with Mummy and get the cookies. Then we can have a proper tea party. How does that sound?'

Hope considered the question for a split second. She clearly wanted to go with Holly, but as Anne had already learned, arranging her teddies for tea parties was something Hope loved doing. Doing it with real people was even better.

'Okay,' Hope said with a nod. 'Nanny and Mamma get shortbread.'

Holly wasn't sure why Anne wanted the two to be alone together. She briefly considered that Anne might be cross with her for making a scene with Giles, but that didn't seem like the Anne she knew. Still, Holly found no answers in the silence that consumed them as she followed her through the house. Only when they reached the kitchen did Anne stop and turn to look at Holly.

'I think I might have been selfish here,' she said, breaking the silence with the last words Holly expected to hear.

'What? Why? No.' From what she had already seen of Anne, she knew she was as selfless as a person could come. 'Why would you say that?'

'I think your friend's right. I think you're running away from things and, deep down, I've always known that. I've known that from the moment you said you wanted to come to America, and had I been a better person, I would have stopped you. But like I said, I was selfish.'

'Anne, you were not selfish,' Holly said, taking her not-quite-mother-in-law's hands. 'I wanted to come here. Me, alone. And it was the right thing to do.'

'Maybe, but...' She paused and glanced over to the corner of the room where two tub chairs were positioned to look out over the forest beyond. 'Can I tell you something? Something I don't talk about very often? Not very often at all, actually.'

No matter how much Holly wanted to run back into the dining room and hide away with Hope, or better still, get straight back on a plane so that she wouldn't have to face the memorial the next day, or the flight back with Giles, she knew there was only one answer she could give.

'Of course,' she said. 'Of course you can.'

77

Tension had taken hold of Holly. Her legs, arms, everything felt rigid as she sat on the seat and waited to hear whatever it was Anne wanted to tell her.

'Did you know triplets run in our family?' she said, only to shake her head. 'No, why would you? Evan didn't know that. Only Catherine knew until last week. That was when Jonathan told the rest of the girls what had happened. He thought I should be the one to do it, but I wasn't there, and I felt they needed to know. I thought it would help them make sense, and see that there is still a way forward. We still haven't talked about it properly, though, but I'm sure we will.'

Holly wasn't sure she fully understood what Anne was trying to tell her, but she was certain there would be a point to it, and so she remained silent.

'I was one of three,' Anne continued. 'Though it was the other way around to mine. Two boys and me. Crazy, isn't it? I guess that's why Evan was always so special. Not because he was the only boy, but because part of him reminded me of myself. Of being that odd one out.'

She drew in a deep breath, and tears glazed her eyes. Other than when Holly had caught her, late at night, flicking through the photo album, Holly felt it was the most vulnerable she had seen Anne appear since they'd arrived in Seattle. As she sat there, the tension rising through her spine and neck, Holly had a horrible feeling she knew how this story ended, and she didn't want to hear it, but she knew she couldn't stop Anne from talking. She had no right to do that.

'It was a car accident,' Anne said. 'Four of them were in the boys' car. All lost their lives, pretty much instantly. They'd been to a party. The driver of their car wasn't drinking, but the other one was. They were less than a mile away from home when it happened.'

'Anne, I'm so sorry,' Holly said, reaching out and taking her hand.

Anne smiled meekly.

'I always say that it was Catherine's dad who was the deadbeat, and he was, don't get me wrong. But I wasn't much better. I just wanted to block it all out. I needed to. In that one moment, I lost my identity. We were seventeen, we were meant to be starting the most exciting stage of our lives, and then they were gone. Can you even be a triplet when the other two no longer exist?'

The way Anne posed the question made it sound like she actually wanted Holly to give her an answer, but there was nothing Holly could say, and so she remained silent.

'It's taken me a long time to accept that I'm not betraying them by not telling people about them,' Anne said. 'And I'm sure the girls will be a little hurt that I kept this part of my life hidden, but it was what I needed to do. I needed to put them away, hide that part of my life. Otherwise, I would never have been able to start anew. I would never have had this amazing family. But sometimes I wish... I wish I hadn't let them fade from my mind so much. I wish I hadn't pushed it all away. I just thought the memories would be there forever, hurting me, haunting me, but now so many have faded, gone altogether, and I would do anything to get them back.'

As she wiped away her tears, Holly knew she wasn't talking solely about her brothers, but about Evan, too. Memories of his childhood that may have long since faded away. Memories she was desperate to hold on to. That was why they had watched the school plays and why she'd been flicking through the photo albums: to find those memories again.

With a sharp sniff, Anne looked Holly straight in the eye.

'I don't know what the next year will be like for you, or the next ten, but I know it won't be easy. You will be reminded of him all the time. And people will get things wrong. Your friends will make mistakes. Your family too. My parents withdrew so much, it was like they couldn't bear to see me because I reminded them of what they had lost. My friends didn't know how to talk to me, and so many of them just stopped trying. If it hadn't been for Jonathan...'

She paused and shuddered, as if recalling a future she had been spared from.

'Feel it, Holly. Let yourself feel that grief, because as wrong as it may feel, that grief would not be there without the love that came before it. You wouldn't feel it so deeply had you not loved him so fiercely. So allow yourself to feel that grief. And allow your friends to be there for you when you do. Of course, this is just an old woman's advice, but it's advice I intend to live by too. I can promise you that.'

Anne sat back in her seat, and Holly knew she had said all she wanted to, yet as Holly breathed in, she was surprised to find the taste of tears at the back of her throat. She hadn't even realised she had been crying, and she certainly didn't know who she had been crying for. Gently, she brushed them away and looked at her not-quite-mother-in-law, still struggling to know what to say.

Thankfully, Anne had the exact right words.

'Come on. Hope will be waiting for those shortbreads,' she said.

.

78

Picking out an outfit to wear for such an occasion felt futile. What did it matter what she wore? There were going to be dozens of people there who didn't know her and would probably look at her and wonder why someone as amazing as Evan had chosen to be with someone as ordinary as her. And they would be right in questioning it. It wasn't like she knew either. In the end, though, Holly opted for a dark-green, woollen dress with tights and boots. She had let Hope choose an outfit from the bag given by Melissa and as such she was wearing a sparkly gold tutu with a dinosaur jumper. She had also wanted to wear a pair of glittery shoes that were two sizes big for her, and Holly's refusal had led to tears. And so, in need of a peaceful life, today of all days, Holly had stuffed tissue down to the toes of the shoes and tried to make them fit a little better. Now Hope was hobbling along, clearly uncomfortable but refusing to give in and take the shoes off. Holly was just grateful Ben wasn't there to see it.

Downstairs, Catherine was sitting with Parker and Mel's two, giving them breakfast.

'What time to we need to get to the hall?' Holly said, plonking

Hope down on a seat next to Lauren within easy reach of the pancakes.

'We said for people to start arriving at the hall after twelve thirty, ready for the memorial at one,' Catherine answered. 'So I think Mum and Dad want to leave about twelve.'

Holly glanced up at the clock. 'Three hours,' she said.

'Three hours,' Catherine replied. Holly assumed she was thinking the same thing as she was. Three hours of just waiting. Although Holly did have one job to do.

Since Anne had first asked her to speak at the memorial, Holly had been planning what to say, and she had so far come up with one line. It was a good line, in her opinion. It was true and heart-felt, and she suspected the people at the memorial would know that, but it was hardly a eulogy. She needed a proper speech and yet she didn't know where to start. So, as Hope helped herself to a second pancake, Holly turned to Catherine.

'You don't mind if I disappear for a bit, do you? I need to figure out what to say.'

'You go for it,' Catherine replied. 'All the others are going to be here in a bit. We can look after Hope. Take all morning if you want. We all want to get as much Hope time as possible in before you leave tonight.'

'Thank you. I think it might take me a while.'

Back upstairs in the bedroom, Holly realised it wasn't a case of time. She just didn't know what to write.

How could you put into words what someone like Evan brought to the world? How could she explain to people who had never seen the pair of them together how he made her feel? She didn't know where to even begin with such a mammoth task and so, at quarter to eleven when the doorbell rang, she decided that maybe staring at a blank page wasn't the best idea, and perhaps a little break would help.

'I'll go get it,' Melissa yelled from downstairs. A moment later, she called again. 'Holly, it's for you.'

Holly knew there was only one person it could be, but she wasn't ready to speak to him. Not after the day before. Even after what Erin had said to her, she couldn't quite face Giles yet, and yet for some reason, having stormed out of their house the day before, he was now standing there in front of her.

79

Holly's teeth ground together. All the anger she'd somehow pushed aside overnight began bubbling inside. She wanted to remember everything Anne had told her the night before, about friends making mistakes and feeling her grief, but it was hard with Giles there staring at her. All she could think was that he was judging her. Judging her at a time when she needed it the least.

'What are you doing here?' she asked. 'I thought you said we'd see each other on the plane. You made that pretty clear when you left.'

'I know,' Giles answered. 'But I'd forgotten you had the memorial. I'm sorry. I wasn't thinking properly.'

He paused, as if he was expecting Holly to say something, but he was the one who had turned up on the doorstep, so as far as Holly was concerned, he was the one who should do all the talking. For a moment longer, Giles waited, looking at Holly expectantly, until he finally gave in and carried on talking.

'I was thinking about Hope,' he said. 'Well, you and Hope. I'm guessing you don't want to have her there during the readings and things. I thought I could help. Just be on hand, you know, look after her so you can do whatever you need to.'

'She's got plenty of family here,' Holly said, her jaw locked. 'We're fine.'

'I know she's got family here,' Giles said. His voice was uncharacteristically measured, as if he was having to keep his temper, too.

Holly's mind flickered to their conversation the night before. The comments she had thrown at him. They were bound to have hurt on some level, but hadn't he deserved it? Possibly not, she admitted to herself. Although it didn't make the anger fade. No, it smouldered away, a consistent simmer.

Holly wanted to be truthful with herself. To admit that she wasn't just angry with Giles, she was angry with the world, the same way Erin had been when she took it all out on Holly. But if she opened up to that anger, where would it leave her? Where would it leave Hope?

'I know Evan's family is Hope's, too,' Giles carried on. 'But today is going to be tough for them. I'm sure they need their own space to grieve and think. What happens if Hope wants you when you're doing your speech? Or she gets upset while you're standing there? Are you just going to walk away? This is not me *slipping* into anyone's place, by the way. This is me being a friend and someone Hope can trust. That's all.'

Holly wanted to tell him to leave. Tell him that she didn't want him there, a constant reminder of the world back home that would never be the same. She wanted to tell him she regretted so many things she had said the night before, while he had been spot on with almost everything he said. Holly wanted to say that she was sorry, but she couldn't find the words.

Instead, what she said was, 'Fine, you can help with Hope. Just stay out of my way.'

80

A few dozen people. That was what Anne and Jonathan had said about the memorial. Forty, maybe fifty at most. After all, that was how many people the church hall could hold. But every seat was full, as was every scrap of space. The family had reserved the front row of chairs, while Giles had already taken a seat right at the back. Holly didn't know who had brought him, just like she didn't know how he had got back to the hotel the evening before, but she hadn't asked. She was too busy for that, what with helping everyone bring sandwiches and drinks in, not to mention being introduced to dozens of people who offered her condolences.

'I'm so sorry for your loss,' one man said, squeezing Holly's hand so tightly, her knuckles clicked. 'He was a good man. A great man.'

'Yes, yes he was,' Holly said.

'I was meant to come out and see him, you know. Always said I would. Always promised myself that when I was a bit less busy at work, or had a bit more money in the bank, I'd make the trip. But I never did. I guess I'll never get over the pond now.'

Holly wasn't sure how to respond. After all, she wasn't sure what the man was sadder about. The fact Evan was gone, or the fact he had missed his chance of a holiday in England. And so she said nothing at all and waited for him to move on.

While Holly continued to thank people for their best wishes, Hope was happy enough playing with her new cousins. When the speeches began, they were all asked to take a seat.

Emily started. She was the sister that Holly had spoken to the least over the trip, but the way she spoke about Evan left Holly in no doubt that they would stay in touch. Perhaps she would try to arrange a trip somewhere with her and Erin. Somewhere they could meet that wasn't too much travelling for either side, though she didn't know where that would be.

'That time, after he got me down, he made me promise never to climb trees ever again, saying he wouldn't rescue me again if I did. Obviously, the next day, you can imagine exactly where I went.'

The congregation let out a light chuckle, and as Holly glanced to her side, she saw most of the people were brushing a tear from their eyes. She pulled in a deep breath and straightened her spine. It wouldn't do any good if she crumbled now.

After Emily finished her speech, it was time for Catherine to read a poem, although it wasn't the normal type of poem you heard read out at these types of events. It was an acrostic poem, written by Evan when he was nine years old, dedicated to the word 'family'. Anne had found it in her box from the attic and decided she wanted to get it framed to go in the house, but it was Catherine who suggested they read it at the memorial first. And it was certainly a good choice, in Holly's opinion, at least.

'F is for friends, which we're all meant to be. A is for adults, who can do what they please. M is for Mom. With Dad, she's our world. I is for individual boy with loads of girls. L is for love, which holds us together. Y is for you lot, who I'll be stuck with forever.'

The congregation laughed again as yet more tears flowed. You could hear Evan's humour and wit in his words. Even from such a young age, he'd had the ability to charm everyone. And yet he had chosen her. He had chosen Holly as the person he wanted to spend the rest of his life with.

'Holly?'

Holly blinked. The hall was entirely silent, as if it was waiting for something, while Catherine was looking at her expectantly. And not just Catherine. All along their row, the family's gaze had turned to her.

With a sudden drop in her stomach, Holly realised what everyone was waiting for. It was her turn to speak.

81

Holly's heart drummed in her chest as sweat clammed across her skin. She regretted the choice of the woollen dress now. She hadn't realised how warm it would be, how claustrophobic she would find it all. But it was just a small speech. That was all Anne had asked for, and that was all she'd written. Just a few lines long. All she needed to do was get through them, and that would be it. It would be over. In less than twelve hours, she would be boarding a plane. Back to... back to what?

She fought the thought down and took her place at the stand. With her hand trembling, she looked down at the piece of paper she was holding.

'Evan... Evan...' Holly cleared her throat. A strange tickle was stopping the words from coming out. When she tried to say his name for a third time, she managed nothing but a slight squeak. Emily and Catherine had spoken so eloquently. So easily, even. And now she was going to let them all down. With a cough into her hand, Holly glanced back down at the words, and started again.

'Evan was loved by everyone who met him...' she said, relieved to finally get something out. That was where she had started. The one line she had known she wanted to say, and she wished more than anything that she could leave it at that. She wished that that single line would be enough, but she knew it wasn't. So swallowing back the lump that had taken the place of the itchiness in her throat, Holly steadied herself against the lectern and carried on.

'Evan was loved by everyone, but I didn't want to love him when I met him.'

The image flooded into her mind. That first flash of smile in an airport bar. That first glass of bubbles that he'd poured for her.

'I didn't want to fall for him, with his smile that lit up a room, and his charm that could sweep anyone off their feet. I didn't want to, because I didn't think he would ever fall for someone like me. Not really. Because he is so special. Was.' She corrected herself. 'Was so special.'

The lump was back again, and this time took longer to swallow down.

'I never felt special in my life until Evan,' she said, following the script she had written for herself. 'Because that's the thing Evan can do better than anyone else. He makes you feel like you're the most important and wonderful person in the world. He makes... he made... made. He made me feel like I was the most important.'

There was something about the use of the past tense that was tripping her up. It didn't sound right. It wasn't right. Not in front of all these people. She didn't want to speak like that. She didn't want to speak like that at all. Her eyes were blurring as she struggled to the paper, but it didn't matter. She could remember, couldn't she? She could remember what she wanted to say.

'It wasn't just me Evan loved, though,' Holly said, feeling her breaths grow shallower and shallower with every word she spoke.

'My daughter, Hope, he loved with his whole heart. God, he loved her. He loved her... and... he was... he was...'

She couldn't seem to get any air into her lungs, and every time she tried to say another word, the tears spilled down from her cheeks.

'He was... He's gone... He's gone... and I don't know what I'm meant to do any more. I don't know... I don't know.'

She could feel her knees giving. Her head spinning. The heat of the hall suffocating her. Holly knew she needed to get off the stage and away from all those pitying eyes. She needed to leave, but she couldn't.

'I... I...' The tears were so thick now, she couldn't even make out where the steps down to the ground were. She would trip and fall and there would be no one to catch her. Not now Evan was gone. She was wheezing, and turning in a circle, lost in the moment, when a hand reached out and took hers.

'It's okay, Holly. I've got you. I've got you,' Giles said, as he pulled her close and wrapped her against his chest.

'He's gone, Giles,' she whispered, rocking back and forth as he held her. 'I don't know what to do... I don't know what I'm supposed to do.'

82

Holly had asked Giles to drive her straight from the airport to Ben's house. The emergency work that Ben had needed to be back in England for had been solved in forty-eight hours, and he was desperate to see Hope again, given how upset she'd been when they parted in America. Although they were barely two miles out of the airport when Hope fell asleep, and there was nothing Holly could do to wake her. As such, Holly suspected Ben was going to be in for a rough night with very little sleep, but she warned him via text and he still insisted that Hope came to his.

'I'll pop in and see Jamie and Fin and then I can take you back to your house whenever you're ready,' Giles said as they drove down the Fosseway towards Bourton.

'Actually,' Holly said, 'I've already messaged Jamie. I'm going to stay there tonight.'

'You are?'

Holly nodded. 'It's just for tonight. Until Anne and the others get here. Then I'll go back to my place with Hope and Evan's sisters. I think that will be better than staying at home on my own. I think it will be good to have people around me.'

Holly paused, noting the way Giles was looking at her with his eyes narrowed, almost as if in curiosity.

'What?' she said. 'You think I'm doing the wrong thing?'

'No,' Giles said, shaking his head. 'I think you're doing exactly the right thing. I think you're letting your friends look after you. And that's all they've wanted to do, from the very start of this, Holly. That's all any of us want to do.'

'I get it. It's just not as easy as I thought it would be.'

'Well, maybe it would get easier if you gave it some practice,' Giles suggested.

At Ben's house, Holly handed over Hope, then unloaded a couple of bags from the back of the car.

'Do you want to stay for a drink?' Jamie asked Giles. 'Or you can stay the night if you want? I can pull out the sofa bed. The more the merrier and all that.'

Giles shook his head. 'Thank you, but no. I need to get back. I've got to be up early in the morning, but I'll probably pop down later in the day, if that's okay with you.'

'Always.'

After hugging Fin, Giles kissed Jamie goodbye and went to do the same to Holly, only she stopped him.

'I'll walk you out,' she said.

Just as she had offered, Holly walked Giles out to his car, only to wish she'd had the foresight to grab her coat first. It wasn't as cold as Seattle, but the air was still biting, and she folded her arms around herself, trying to keep her body warm.

'What are you doing? Go inside,' Giles said. 'We didn't get you all the way from America and back safely for you to die of hypothermia out here.' The minute he realised what he had said, his face turned ashen. 'Holly, God. I'm so sorry. I'm so—'

Holly shook her head. 'Don't. You don't need to apologise.'

'I mean, what I just said—'

'I know. It was a slip of the tongue. It'll happen. The things I said to you, on the other hand…'

Holly had spent several hours on the plane, considering how she should apologise to Giles, writhing in the guilt of how cruel she had been to him. But now, even after all that contemplation, she was still struggling to find the words.

'Giles, I said some horrible things to you. Things you didn't deserve.'

'Holly, we don't need to do this. Go inside. It's freezing.'

'I know, I know, but I just need to say this. I just need to get it off my chest. I'm so sorry. I know you were only trying to be a friend. To be my best friend, and that's what you are. That's what you've become, so I'm so grateful to you. I want you to know that because I think, I think over the next few months, I'm going to have other times like that. Other days where maybe I say things that are cruel or hurtful, because I'm angry, Giles, I'm angry with the whole world.'

'You have every right to be, Holly,' Giles said softly.

'Maybe, but I'm sorry that I took it out on you. And if it happens again, I'm sorry for that too. Please don't let it push you away. I need you in my life, Giles. No matter what I say, I need you.'

Without a word, Giles stepped forward, wrapped his arms around Holly, and pulled her into his chest.

'You don't need to apologise to me,' he said. 'And you don't ever need to worry about losing me. You'll never push me away.'

'Promise?' Holly said.

'Promise.'

83

'I can't believe how many people there are,' Fin said to Holly. The pair stood by the door to the church, welcoming people in, although all the seating room had gone and people were having to stand at the back. Considering how Evan had only lived in Bourton for a couple of years, Holly was amazed how many people turned up for the funeral. There were friends and colleagues from London, of course, not to mention dozens of customers who Evan had met when helping at the shop.

Given the number of people they had to cram into the church, the service didn't get started until ten minutes later than planned, but Holly wasn't stressed about timings. It wasn't a big deal. What mattered was making sure everyone who wanted to say goodbye to Evan got the chance.

They began with a welcome given by Jonathan, then at Holly's request, Erin read Evan's poem about family, while Fin's eulogy, which included tales from the past and from a future Evan would never know, had the congregation crying and laughing at various points.

And then it was Holly's turn.

Holly took to the lectern slowly, taking her time to place her piece of paper in front of her as she looked at the sea of faces. Her throat was tight, and there was a slight tremble to her knees, but she knew it didn't matter what her voice sounded like or how much she wanted to cry. She would be doing this speech in full. She would be giving Evan the farewell he deserved.

'I had a bit of practice in America, doing a speech like this for Evan's family and friends over there, and it didn't go very smoothly.' With her heart hammering against her ribs, she paused before she carried on. 'So, this time, I thought I would take a leaf out of Evan's book, because it's a sign of how talented he was that the poem he wrote when he was eight was better than anything I could come up with as an adult.' This time, there was a slight chuckle from the congregation. Holly smiled and looked out at all the people who had come there to say goodbye to Evan. Even though it felt unnatural, she held her expression for a moment longer before taking a deep breath in and continuing.

'So, like I said, I'm going to take my lead from Evan and the reading you just heard his sister do. A poem that Evan wrote around the word family. I've never been particularly good at poetry, but I thought I would try to do the same. My poem for Evan, just like the one he wrote, is called "Family".'

She had written the poem on the flight back to England, with no intention of ever sharing it. The words had simply formed in her head and, as Hope slept on her shoulder, Holly had scribbled them down. So far, no one other than Anne and Jonathan had heard it, and they had both thought it was perfect for the occasion. Still, it was more than a little nerve-wracking, sharing something this personal. With one last breath in, and a brief smile at her mother, Holly began.

'F is forever, which I thought we would be, and a
    lifetime of places I dreamed we would see.

'A is for anger, which burns in my heart, because
    our time was over before it could start.

'M is for magnificent, because my darling you were.
    You were a hero, a best friend, a brother, and
    our world.

'I is for infinite as my love is for you, and yours was
    for us. We were lucky, it's true.

'L is for laughter, which once filled our home. I
    keep trying to smile now, but it's hard on
    my own.

'Y is for yesterdays, when the sun used to shine. It's
    all gone quite dark now, but at least you were
    mine.'

84

Holly had offered the spare room to Anne and Jonathan for as long as they wanted it, and it appeared as though they had genuinely considered the idea of staying longer. But they wanted to get back for the girls, and Holly understood that. Hope needed a new normality, and Holly needed to be the one to provide that, in whatever form she could.

'You know you're welcome, anytime,' Anne said. 'You just turn up on our doorstep and there'll be a bed for you. You know that?'

'Thank you,' Holly said, pulling Evan's mother in close for one last tight hug, before moving on to Jonathan.

'Look after that granddaughter of mine, won't you?' he said.

'I will, and look after each other, won't you?' Holly said. 'I think we're all going to have some bad days in the future, but we just need to look to each other to pull us out of them.'

Her hugs to Emily and Ashley were similarly swift, but it was when she reached Erin that Holly found herself struggling most of all.

'We'll see each other again soon,' Erin said, speaking as she sniffed back the tears. 'I think Evan's ghost would kick our butts if we don't.'

'I'm pretty sure you're right.'

Holly stepped back and let Fin take her place in offering his final hugs to the family. He had come with her to the airport, and Holly was grateful. With all the people and luggage, they'd had to hire a minibus, and there was no way she would have managed that on her own.

After finally waving the family through into departures, Fin and Holly made their way back to the car.

'So, where do you want dropping?' Fin said, as they travelled down the Fosseway. 'At your house, or did you want to go get Hope from Ben's first?'

'Hope's staying at Ben's tonight,' Holly said. The words alone were enough to cause a twinge in her chest. Hope had stayed with her the entire time Evan's family had been over, so they'd got to spend as much time with her as possible and Ben had been very good about it, although Holly knew how much he had missed Hope. Now she was losing everyone in one fell swoop.

'Actually,' Holly said. 'Would you mind dropping me at the sweet shop?'

'The shop? Are you sure? You know it's gone six, right?'

Holly nodded. She hadn't been in for weeks now, and though she knew the others had done an amazing job of keeping everything up to date, she wanted to get a quick check on how everything was going before she started back at work over the weekend. That was the plan at least, although when she stepped through the door, she found herself struck with a thousand memories. Not of Evan, but of the sweet shop and the way she'd found it all those years ago, when Maud had let the place fall into disrepair, as she struggled to keep going through the grief of losing Agnes.

Holly got it now. She got how these jars and sweets didn't seem to have purpose or meaning. Not next to something as big as love and loss, but as that thought entered, so did another. Like the way the sweet shop had kept her going and given her a whole new lease of life after Dan's cheating. As she closed her eyes, Holly thought about how the shop had brought Caroline and Jamie and everyone she now held so close into her life. She thought of the customers, who came in week after week, not for the sweets as such, but for the meanings of the sweets. Memories of childhoods, treats for grandchildren. Gifts for loved ones. The sweet shop was more than just bricks and mortar. It was more than just sugar and chocolate. It was a refuge. A comfort, and a spark of love and light in what was sometimes a grey and sad world.

It had brought her back from that place before, and she knew now that with Hope by her side, it would pull her through this time, too.

ACKNOWLEDGEMENTS

This was a tricky book to write. It wasn't until I started plotting that I realised what was going to happen and it's safe to say I shed quite a few tears! But don't despair, I promise Holly will get her happy ever after and it will not be snatched away from her again.

I am enormously grateful to all my readers who have come on this journey with me. Both Holly and I have had a fair few adventures since I started this series all those years ago, and that would not have been possible without your support. I'm sorry if this one was a bit more of a tear jerker than normal, but I can assure you that in the next book in the series – which will be the final one – there will only be happy tears!

I owe a lot of thanks to my editor Emily, who helped me find the right tone and balance for this book and to the team at Boldwood Books for their support.

As always, I want to thank Nina, the real-life sweet shop owner, for giving a teenage me my first Saturday job. Who knew that this is where it would lead!

To my family and friends who have infinite patience when I'm in a plotting mindset, during which I struggle to hold a conversation, thank you for putting up with me. None of my stories would exist without Jake's endless support and I am so grateful I picked you to spend my life with.

With all that said, I want to offer one last thanks to my readers, because without you, I would not be able to create these stories and it is such a privilege to do. Thank you.

ABOUT THE AUTHOR

Hannah Lynn is the author of over twenty books spanning several genres. Hannah grew up in the Cotswolds, UK. After graduating from university, she spent 15 years as a teacher of physics, teaching in the UK, Thailand, Malaysia, Austria and Jordan.

Sign up to Hannah Lynn's mailing list here for news, competitions and updates on future books.

Visit Hannah's website: www.hannahlynnauthor.com

Follow Hannah on social media:

facebook.com/hannahlynnauthor
instagram.com/hannahlynnwrites
tiktok.com/@hannah.lynn.romcoms
bookbub.com/authors/hannah-lynn

ALSO BY HANNAH LYNN

The Holly Berry Sweet Shop Series

The Sweet Shop of Second Chances

Love Blooms at the Second Chances Sweet Shop

High Hopes at the Second Chances Sweet Shop

Family Ties at the Second Chances Sweet Shop

Sunny Days at the Second Chances Sweet Shop

A Summer Wedding at the Second Chances Sweet Shop

Snowflakes Over the Second Chances Sweet Shop

The Wildflower Lock Series

New Beginnings at Wildflower Lock

Coffee and Cake at Wildflower Lock

Blue Skies Over Wildflower Lock

LOVE NOTES

LOVE IN EVERY CHAPTER

WHERE ALL YOUR ROMANCE
DREAMS COME TRUE!

THE HOME OF BESTSELLING
ROMANCE AND WOMEN'S
FICTION

 WARNING:
MAY CONTAIN SPICE

SIGN UP TO OUR
NEWSLETTER

https://bit.ly/Lovenotesnews

Boldwood

Boldwood Books is an award-winning fiction publishing company seeking out the best stories from around the world.

Find out more at www.boldwoodbooks.com

Join our reader community for brilliant books, competitions and offers!

Follow us
@BoldwoodBooks
@TheBoldBookClub

Sign up to our weekly deals newsletter

https://bit.ly/BoldwoodBNewsletter

Printed in Great Britain
by Amazon

52656527R00165